With

Christmas

Love—

Stephen Murrey

DISCOVERING THE

CHRISTMAS

SPIRIT

by

Stephen Murray

Discovering the Christmas Spirit

Other Works of Fiction by this Author

The Chapel of Eternal Love
Wedding Stories from Las Vegas
www.thechapelofeternallove.com

Return to the Chapel of Eternal Love
Marriage Stories from Las Vegas
www.thechapelofeternallove.com

Murder Aboard the Queen Elizabeth II
www.murderaboardtheqe2.com

Discreetly Yours
www.discreetlyyours.net

Acknowledgements

To my family and friends – RJ, Sue, Maria, Becky and Judy for all their support and encouragement.

To my writer's group – Sue, Nancy and Donelle for all their invaluable advice and suggestions throughout the process.

To Jennifer Hart, harthousecreative.com, for her imaginative and creative cover design.

My heartfelt gratitude to you all.

Table of Contents

CHAPTER 1

Marilyn shivered as she stepped out of the taxicab. She wrapped the red and green scarf tightly around her neck and pulled the woolen hood over her ears. "Please hurry up with my luggage. I have a horrible feeling I've already missed my flight."

The cab driver watched the crisp night air exhaling from Marilyn's mouth as she spoke. "Here you go, Ma'am. Have a Merry Christmas." He placed the Louis Vuitton suitcase at the curb for her. She thrust a $50 bill in his hand. "Thank you. Happy holidays to you, too." She ran along the sidewalk, turned into the small concourse, and headed to the helicopter booth. She was breathless when she arrived at the counter. "My name is Marilyn Weaverston. I hope I haven't missed my flight. There was a car accident in downtown Jackson Hole, and the traffic was horrendous. Here's my ticket and driver's license."

"Don't worry," smiled the attendant, tapping her computer to verify the information. "The flight has been delayed. There's been a blizzard between here and Cody. Apparently, it's over now, but we always like to wait a while just to make sure. Besides, we're still waiting for two other passengers. I'm assuming they've been delayed for the same reason."

"How many passengers will there be on the helicopter?"

"There will be five of you, plus the pilot. The other two passengers are in the coffee shop. Why don't you join them? We'll come and fetch you when the others are here, and we're ready to go. It looks like you could use a coffee or hot chocolate. Just place this on the table." She handed Marilyn a green plastic cone with the number "3" drawn in white.

"I'd prefer a hot toddy — these past few hours have been so stressful," Marilyn smiled, handing her luggage to the attendant. "But, you're right. A hot chocolate will probably do the trick."

She headed to the coffee shop and spotted the other two individuals with green cones in front of them. "Mind if I join you?"

"Oh, not at all. Please do. I'm Fran."

She almost seems relieved I'm here. Perhaps she's had a spat with her husband, Marilyn thought before turning her attention to the gentleman sporting a thick winter coat with a fur collar, seated alongside Fran. "My name is Marilyn. And, you are?"

STEPHEN MURRAY | 3

"Name's Oscar," he replied, without looking up, both hands remained firmly tucked in his coat pockets. Marilyn looked back at Fran, who merely shrugged.

The waitress appeared before Marilyn had time to seat herself. "I'll take a large hot chocolate, hold the whipped cream, please."

"Excuse me." Oscar rose from the table and departed, taking with him a green cone reflecting the number "1".

As soon as he was out of sight, Marilyn looked at Fran. "I hope I didn't interrupt anything."

Fran shook her head. "Not at all. When I came in, there were no available tables, so I asked if I might join him— especially since we were obviously on the same flight. I tried to engage in conversation, but he has been totally tight-lipped, with just one-word answers. I essentially gave up. I was so pleased when you asked if you could sit with us. I was starting to feel really uncomfortable. I'm not sure what his story is."

"Oh, my! And, here I thought he was your husband."

"Heaven's no!" Fran laughed. The serious and somewhat pained expression that had been on her face now gave way to warm, twinkling eyes and a friendly smile. "I just hope I'm not seated next to him on the flight to Cody. It'll be one very boring journey if I am."

Marilyn took an instant liking to Fran. "So, are you heading to Cody to spend Christmas with family?"

The expression on Fran's face became somber. "No. Actually, I'm going to Cody to get away for Christmas. It's not my favorite time of year. How about you?"

Marilyn shifted in her seat. "I'll be spending it with a friend. A very special friend." When the hot chocolate arrived, she immediately took a sip. "Oh, that tastes so good," she said to the waitress while handing her a $5 bill. "Please, keep the change."

The attendant from the reservation desk arrived at the table. "Excuse me, the other passengers have arrived. We're ready for you to board."

Thank you, Lord, thought Marilyn. She did not want to answer any more questions about Christmas. The ladies picked up their purses, both of them carrying their drinks, and headed for the small departure gate. Oscar was already standing at the runway alongside the other two passengers.

Fran eyed them both. I wonder if this is a father and daughter. Of course, these days, it could be a lover and mistress. Age difference certainly doesn't matter anymore. Looks like he could be a dean of a college or maybe a stockbroker. With her kind of face, she could be a model — either that or she's involved in the arts somehow.

"Have a safe flight. Merry Christmas," the flight attendant chirped as she opened the door to the runway. "Please turn in your green plastic cones and dispose of any drink containers." She was concerned as she watched them scurry gingerly across the slippery surface of the jetway in a desperate attempt to climb inside the helicopter out of the bitter cold. The pilot assisted the passengers onto the helicopter, and the flight attendant waited for the departure before heading back to her desk to finalize all the necessary procedure reports.

"Welcome onboard! I'm your captain, Brian McFitten." In his heavy Bostonian accent, he apologized for the late departure. "Weather conditions prohibited us from leaving earlier, but we now have clear skies ahead, and our flight time should be as scheduled. Please relax, keep your seat belts fastened, and enjoy the hour-long flight as we pass over the Grand Teton National Park and part of Yellowstone. There's a full moon tonight, so if the clouds clear up, you might get some spectacular aerial views. Anyone have any questions?"

There was silence among the passengers. *First time I've ever had a flight where no one has any questions or comments. How strange.*

"Would anybody like to lead us with a Christmas carol?" he asked. There were muffled chuckles from the group. The helicopter continued its familiar journey, with only the monotonous constant sound of the engine to pierce the silence.

As the helicopter rose higher, a full moon emerged, and the puffy white clouds drifted aimlessly across the sky, providing breathtaking views of the Tetons. Every now and then, the occasional "Wow" and "Awesome" could be heard from one of the passengers with the ubiquitous clicking of the cameras, as the flight left the Tetons and moved through Yellowstone.

Suddenly, the engine sounded as if it was sputtering, and a rocking motion took effect. Marilyn began to scream.

"What's happening? What's going on?" Oscar demanded with a tinge of panic in his voice.

The captain frantically turned the dials back and forth on the instrument panel as he felt the chopper spiraling downwards. "Mayday! Mayday! Mayday!" he yelled. All of the women were screaming now. Fran saw the unknown male passenger place his arms around the younger lady.

"Repeating: Mayday! Mayday! Mayday! I have to make an emergency landing. There's a field of snow immediately below me. My coordinates are … " His voice trailed off as the helicopter crashed into a large fir tree.

*****

Brian opened his eyes. The groaning sounds of the other passengers flooded his ears. He turned his head slowly, just enough to make sure everyone was alive. They all seemed to be breathing. The glass was shattered, and the cold night air penetrated his jacket. Through the haze, he could see a convoy of headlights on the distant side of the snowy blanket in front of him. *Thank God — help is on the way,* he thought just before he slipped out of consciousness.

CHAPTER 2

"**G**ood morning, Cassie. My name's Gabriel." The voice was warm and friendly. "My husband and I own this hotel. I hope you're feeling a little better this morning. We thought you might enjoy some breakfast." The aroma of fresh coffee permeated the room. Gabriel placed the tray on the table in front of the window, turned and smiled at the young lady lying in bed.

"Hotel? What hotel? I can't afford a hotel! Where in the hell am I?" Cassie bolted upright in bed. "Ouch!" She held her hand to her forehead. "Boy, do I have a doozy of a headache. Wonder where in the world that came from? I don't even remember partying last night."

Gabriel fluffed the pillows behind Cassie's back before sitting on the side of the bed and holding her hand. "Don't worry, my dear. You're just suffering from a mild concussion. You'll be fine in a few days."

Cassie looked at her host. "A few days? Are you kidding me? I don't have a few days — I have to be in Cody for Christmas! What happened? What am I doing in a hotel?" Completely confused, Cassie looked around the room and at the stranger in front of her. "Where am I? Am I in Cody?"

Gabriel started to stroke Cassie's cheek gently. "No, you're not in Cody. Your helicopter crashed in a nearby field. A team of us came to rescue you. You're safe."

"That's right. Now, I remember." Cassie began to calm down as her memory returned. "Are all of the other passengers OK?" A sudden flash of recognition overcame her wide-eyed face. "There was an older guy I was chatting with at the airport gate in Jackson Hole. He reminded me of one of my college professors. He was so nice and comforting when the pilot lost control of the helicopter. He put his arms around me as if he was trying to protect me. You know what I mean? Such a sweet, kind man. I hope he's alright."

Gabriel patted Cassie's hand. "He's fine. All of the passengers are. They're all staying here. The doctor will be stopping by shortly. If he gives his permission, and you're up to it, maybe you'll be able to have dinner with your fellow travelers later."

Cassie panicked as she realized again that she was in a hotel. "But, I'm only a college graduate. I can't afford to stay here. Why didn't they take me to a hospital? You haven't told me where I am. My family can come and get me."

Gabriel headed toward the table where Cassie's breakfast was waiting. "There's no hospital here. You crashed in a small town. You're staying at the Holly and Ivy Hotel in Christmas Carol Village. The nearest hospital is in Cody, but there was a blizzard and the roads are covered in snow. We needed a plow to get to where your accident was last night. Our rescue volunteers helped bring you into town. Of course, that was after Dr. Shepherd made sure there were no broken bones. Fortunately, among all the passengers, there only seems to be a few fractures, a concussion, and a couple of sprains. You're all very fortunate. The Gods were smiling down on you. Now, why don't you come have breakfast before it gets cold?"

"I'm not too sure I would agree with your comments about the Gods," Cassie grumbled as she slowly shifted her legs sideways, attempting to slide gently out of bed. Gabriel helped her toward the table and parted the drapes.

"I'll leave you to enjoy your breakfast, but I'll be back to check on you later." She smiled at her guest and left the room.

Cassie looked at the tray in front of her and, suddenly, her taste buds awoke at the sight of scrambled eggs, hash browns, sausage links, and buttered wheat toast. She poured herself a cup of coffee, and as she set the carafe down, the corner of her eye caught the window.

"Oh, my goodness," she cried. "What a magnificent sight!" The view from her room overlooked what was clearly the town center. The words "Poinsettia Plaza" were carved out of wood in large letters and placed at the edge of the sidewalk. From corner to corner, the ground came alive with the familiar holiday bloom. In the center of the square stood the tallest Christmas tree she had ever seen. It was adorned with an abundance of the largest red baubles imaginable and the brightest star in the sky. From each corner, a snow-covered, narrow concrete path led to the tree.

Torn between the feeling of utter starvation and absolute wonder, Cassie grabbed the plate and brought it to the window with her so she could eat while reading the shop names. She smiled at the creativity. For a moment, she almost wished she had more time to spend in this fascinating, quaint spot. But she needed to get to Cody in time for Christmas. She cast her mind away from her anxieties and continued to stare in awe at the view while savoring her meal.

It wasn't long before Gabriel knocked on the door. For the first time, Cassie actually noticed her matronly

STEPHEN MURRAY | 13

host. Her hair was short and had begun to gray. She was cloaked in a floor-length, green dress that was almost entirely hidden by her apron. *How fitting*, she thought, and smiled.

"You really are an angel," Cassie said, as she admired the cherubs that covered the apron, pausing on each one to notice the facial expression. "And you must forgive me. I haven't even said thank you. I don't know how I'm going to pay you for my stay. I've just noticed the nightgown I'm wearing. It's not even mine."

Gabriel shook her head. "Now, my dear, you're not to worry about a thing. That's a cute nightie, though, isn't it?" she asked, as Cassie looked down at the warm, winter gown to see a large print of Santa Claus waving his gloved hand. "Obviously, you can't see it, but on the back there's a picture of Mrs. Claus holding a tin of cookies," she said with a chuckle. "They were brought over here last night with some pajamas for the men from the Wisemans. They're the owners of Festive Fashions, our local clothing store. The extra blankets for the bed were provided by the Garlands, the owners of Yule Love It Linens.

"How can I repay these kind people? We're all complete strangers to them." Cassie looked at the quilt and quickly recognized that the square patches featured the eight reindeer immortalized in "A Visit from St. Nicholas" by Clement Clark Moore. She shook her head.

"There's nothing to repay. Life is about giving. That's what we do here. We try to give back and give of ourselves. Now, why don't you go back to bed and get some rest? Your body has had quite a shock, you know. The doctor will be here shortly. He's visiting the other passengers right now." She made her way to the table and helped Cassie toward the bed.

"No, I can't rest. I must get dressed and be ready to leave."

Gabriel put her arms around her guest. "You're not going anywhere right now. There's another blizzard coming. You're likely to be here for another couple of days at least. The roads to Cody are already covered with snow from last night. There's no way you'll make it there if another storm comes through."

Cassie thought about the heavy snow from the blizzard and wondered how the poinsettias survived without a single snowflake to be found.

As if reading her mind, Gabriel laughed. "We should probably plant poinsettias up and down both sides of the road from here to Cody. Somehow, for all the snow and cold we get, the poinsettias in the plaza only get a tiny smattering. The tree looks stunning when they're covered with snow. But, the flowers, they look fresh all year round."

"You mean the poinsettias last all year long? Even in the summer?"

"Yes, all year long. It's a beautiful plaza, isn't it?"

"That's amazing. And the tree? What about the Christmas tree? It's magnificent. Is that there all year long too?" Cassie asked, bewildered.

"Well, not exactly. It's changed every three months. Each store in the town square takes turns putting up a new one and takes care of it while it's on display. We all volunteer to help trim it every time, though, and afterwards, everyone comes here for some glühwein."

"What's that?"

"It's a wonderful heated, red wine that's served with cinnamon sticks. We add some special herbs and spices. It's my secret recipe," Gabriel confided.

"Sounds like you celebrate Christmas all year."

"No, we don't actually celebrate it," the host said, as her brow knitted in a pensive manner. "We just try and live it all year long."

Cassie climbed into bed, a frown on her face. Gabriel pulled the comforter over the petite young woman. "What's troubling you, my dear?"

The young guest shrugged. "I'm heading to Cody to see my father and his wife, Heather. I haven't spoken to my dad in several years — not since I started college. It was Heather's idea for me to come, and I agreed in a moment of weakness. I know I need to be there, but I must confess, I'm not exactly looking forward to it." She shook her head.

Gabriel ran her hand gently through Cassie's long, wavy hair, sensing her anxiety. "Whatever is meant to happen will happen. Everything will come right when it is meant to. You'll see. Now, you're not to worry. Try and get some rest, and I'll be here when Dr. Shepherd pays you a visit. By the way, your luggage had your destination address on it. We took the liberty of contacting the police department in Cody. I assume they have already informed your family." She turned and left.

Cassie quietly stared at the ceiling, pondering her situation.

CHAPTER 3

"**C**ome in," hollered Fran, as she heard the knock on her hotel room door. Like Cassie, she was sitting near the window marveling at the view of Poinsettia Plaza. She turned to see who her visitor was and smiled when she saw a young, angelic-looking boy at the doorway clutching a basket in his hands. Fran was struck by his ruddy complexion and blond, tousled hair.

"Excuse me, Miss. Is your name Fran?" he asked.

"Well, that depends on who's doing the asking," she teased. "And what a neat sweater you're wearing. It looks so warm, and I just love the Nativity scene."

The boy looked at the sling around her shoulder. "Gee, Miss. Did you get that from the helicopter crash? It looks mighty painful."

"Fortunately, it's not as painful as it looks. The doctor stopped by this morning, and it's just a small fracture. But you still didn't tell me what your name is and what you want." Fran smiled.

"Oh, I'm sorry, Miss. My name's Noel. And if your name is Fran, then these are yours!" Fran noticed the enthusiasm in his voice as he walked to the table near the window where she was sitting and placed the basket in front of her. "It's a get-well gift from Mr. and Mrs. Hollyberry, owners of The Gingerbread House. We make the best cookies in town and, well … everywhere else too!"

Fran was touched. The basket contained an assortment of holiday cookies shaped like reindeer, Christmas trees, Santa's sleigh, and snowmen. "How very sweet and thoughtful. Where is the shop? I'd like to stop by and thank them."

"Oh, you don't need to do that. They're giving these packages to everyone who was in the helicopter crash. But, if you want to see the store, it's across Poinsettia Plaza. Turn left on Candy Cane Lane, and we're the third shop on the right."

Fran chuckled as he told her the names of the streets. "And what are you doing delivering these cookies? Shouldn't you be in school?"

"Nah. School's out for Christmas break. That's when I work for the Hollyberrys." He put his hands in his pockets and began kicking the foot of the table with his sneakers.

"And just how old are you, Noel?"

The young man looked embarrassed and cast his head downward. "I'll be ten years old on Christmas Day. That's where I got my dumb name from ... Noel."

Fran bit her lip as she fought back the tears. Her voice trembled a little. "That's nice for you. Your birthday is always a holiday, and you'll never have to go to school."

"No, it's not nice to have your birthday on Christmas Day. You get stiffed out of presents. I always get combined birthday and Christmas gifts. It's not fair." His face took on a boyish pout.

"Sit a while, Noel." Fran gestured to the chair across the table. Noel flopped down. "Have you ever considered just how fortunate you are? Have you ever wondered about all those ten-year-old children who never get anything on their birthdays or at Christmas?"

Noel thought for a moment. "Yeah, I guess so. It still doesn't seem fair though."

"I'm sure your parents do the best they can."

Noel continued kicking his feet against the table, his sneakers making a repetitive sound. "I don't have a mom and dad. They were both killed in a car accident when I was six months old. I don't even remember them."

Fran was taken aback. "Then, who takes care of you?" She found this little boy endearing.

"Right now, Mr. and Mrs. Hollyberry. I've had several foster parents, but they've been the longest. They're looking for another foster home for me though. Mrs. Hollyberry is going to have her fourth baby, and they won't have room for me anymore. I'm not sure what is going to happen to me." He wiped away a tear from his eye.

Fran reached across the table and grabbed his hand. "I'm sure something will turn up for you, and it will be for the better."

"It's hard not having a family. Do you have one, Miss — a family?"

"Well, yes and no. I don't have siblings, and I'm divorced."

"I can't imagine why anyone would divorce a pretty lady like you, Miss."

"My husband divorced me because he wanted a family, and I was unable to give him one." She held both his hands in hers. "On Christmas Day, my son would have been ten years old, just like you. The doctors couldn't save him at birth, and I can't have any more children. But the son I lost is my family. He's in my heart and with me all the time. Your parents are with you all the time too, Noel. Just remember that."

Noel stared at his newfound friend. "Would you mind if I gave you a hug?"

Fran chuckled. "Of course not. As long as you're gentle with my right shoulder." She stretched out her left arm, and he wrapped his arms around her neck. She felt his tenderness as he did hers. "You'd better run along now, otherwise you'll be in trouble. And we don't want that to happen, do we?"

Noel stepped back and grinned. "No, we don't. But, can I come back and see you if I have some spare time?"

"Of course, Noel. I'd love to see you anytime. And, why don't you call me Fran for the next few days?" He smiled at her, and she smiled back as she watched him head toward the door. As she had done countless times before, she wondered how different her life would have been if her child had survived.

CHAPTER 4

Oscar opened his eyes and glanced around the room. The first thing he noticed was the neatly made empty bed on the other side of the nightstand. As his eyes slowly scanned the room, he saw two giant murals of Santa Claus smiling and waving his white-gloved hand painted on the closet doors across from each bed. *This is like a bad dream. Good grief, where am I?*

Hearing voices outside of the room, he hollered, "Anybody there? Can anyone hear me?" The sound of someone's feet coming toward the room made Oscar try to sit up, but the pain in his leg made him scream in agony. Suddenly, he remembered the helicopter crash.

There was a knock on the door, which was slightly ajar. "May I come in?" asked the soft-spoken, yet commanding, masculine voice.

"Please do," replied Oscar, anxious to learn more about his injuries and find out where he was staying. Expecting a doctor to enter the room, he was surprised to see a clergyman, dressed in traditional cassock and white collar.

The minister, whom Oscar presumed to be in his mid-fifties, extended his hand. "My name is Father Matthew. I'm so sorry you came to Christmas Carol Village through such unfortunate circumstances." He managed a weak smile.

"It's not your fault, Father," Oscar replied gruffly. "What happened to me though? I'm in so much pain."

The minister sat on the opposite bed. "When the helicopter crashed, all of the passengers were taken to the Holly & Ivy Inn where the local doctor came and tended to everyone's needs."

"So, I'm staying in a hotel?"

"No. Unfortunately, you fractured your right leg, and it will be a while before you can leave. The owners of the inn couldn't keep you there, since it's for an extended period of time. They kept you overnight, and, early this morning, you were transported here, to the Heavenly Home for Disabled Veterans. You were heavily sedated at the time."

Oscar interrupted, "How did anyone know I was a veteran?"

"I understand they found your discharge papers in your wallet when they were looking for your ID. We run a small operation here. There are 20 residents, each sharing a room. You'll be sharing with a very nice young veteran. His name is Andrew. We have a small gym and a professional physical therapist who visits daily. He will help tremendously with your recovery, I would imagine. There's a dining room along the hall where we serve three healthy meals a day."

"And how am I to pay for all this?" Oscar grumbled.

"The Lord will provide," said Father Matthew.

Oscar rolled his eyes. "You're talking to a nonbeliever, Father."

"Well, He always has provided," the minister continued in his good-natured tone. "I've run this place for 15 years. It's like a commune. One of the vets is an excellent chef. Another has a green thumb, so he takes care of the vegetable garden out back. Residents take turns setting the meal tables, washing the dishes, doing the laundry — everyone chips in, and everything gets done."

"Sounds like a real Shangri-La here, Father."

The tone of sarcasm in Oscar's voice was not lost on the minister, who chose to ignore it. "In which war did you serve?" he inquired, deftly changing the subject.

"Vietnam."

"Most of the veterans here served in Desert Storm, the Iraqi war, or in Afghanistan. Many of them suffer from post-traumatic stress disorder. You could be a valuable mentor to them while you're here."

"Yeah? I doubt that. Hey, Father, you don't happen to have a smoke on you, do you?"

"Sorry, son." The minister smiled. "No smoking inside the building, and you're asking the wrong person for a cigarette."

Oscar winced in pain and let out another yell. He reached down to his leg.

"Let me see if I can get the doctor here to give you a shot for that pain. But, don't worry, we'll have you up and about in no time."

"I doubt that as well, Father." Oscar turned away and looked out the window.

"Is there anyone you would like me to call? Any family members? Wife? Children?"

Oscar shook his head. "No, Father. I have no family."

"Friends?"

Oscar shook his head again. "None that I'd like to be contacted."

My fellow sinner sure has a heavy burden he's carrying around. I wish I knew what it was. I suppose it'll be revealed in due course. "Let me fetch that doctor for you. Just yell if you need anything. Someone will hear you." The minister rose from the bedside and left.

CHAPTER 5

Marilyn was lying on her bed in the hotel room, holding her hand to her forehead when the phone rang. She reached out with the other hand to pick up the receiver. "Hello?" she said into the mouthpiece.

"Darling, are you OK? I've been worried sick about you." It was her husband, Richard.

"Oh, I have a splitting headache and my back is sore, but the doctor says I'll be fine. He says I'm just a little bruised."

"I've been trying to call ever since I heard about the helicopter accident, but your cellphone hasn't been working, and I guess the telephone lines have been down. I tried half an hour ago, and they still weren't working."

"Yeah. They told us the lines have been down, and all the roads are blocked."

"I know. I guess they'll be closed until after Christmas. I hate the thought of you being alone on Christmas Day, my precious."

Marilyn smiled. "Accidents happen, and there's nothing we can do about it. I'll be alright. Don't worry."

"You know I'd be right there if I could. I was surprised they had you in a hotel, but then I heard there isn't a hospital close by. Who's taking care of you? Is the hotel comfortable? Sweetheart, I'm just so worried about you."

"Please, I'm telling you, don't worry. The hotel is lovely, and, from what I've seen through my window, Christmas Carol Village is a darling, festive little town. The doctor came by this morning to check on me. And, while I was asleep, a basket of cookies was delivered from a local bakery. Then, the inn owner's wife, Gabriel, stopped by with some breakfast. She's a good-natured soul with a truly giving heart. I'm hoping to go to the dining room tonight to chat with the other passengers on the flight and see how they're doing. But, enough about me. How are the girls?"

"Everyone's fine here in Jackson Hole. We just miss you." He paused. "I guess I'm sorry I agreed to let you go to Cody for Christmas to see your friend. I know she was very ill and needed you, but, if I'd had stood my ground, you'd be here at home — safe. I still think she could have found someone else. Besides, I had a bad feeling from the beginning about that helicopter ride."

If you had stood your ground more often, maybe our marriage wouldn't be in such trouble. "Richard, I appreciate the call and your concern, but my head is really killing me," she said, keeping her thoughts to herself. "I need to take a painkiller and try and get some rest. Would you mind? Now that the phones are working, I can call you later."

"Sure thing, honey. Feel better and take care of yourself. I love you."

"Give my love to the girls, and tell them I miss them." She hung up and reached for the Tylenol and the glass of water on the nightstand. After taking the pill, she picked up the phone again and dialed a number she knew by heart.

"Hello, Eddie."

"Oh, it's you. Thank God. I didn't recognize the number you're calling from and thought it was one of those wretched robocalls," was the curt response.

"Is that all you can say — 'Oh, it's you'?"

"Well, I haven't heard zip from anyone since the police left a note on the door and a message on my voicemail saying you were OK but that you'd been in a plane crash. They mentioned you were being put up at a hotel in a small town somewhere. I've been waiting for you to call."

Marilyn was startled. "Well, you could have tried calling me."

"I did try once, but the cellphones aren't working. Anyway, when and how are you going to get here?"

"Eddie, why do you sound so angry?"

"I just hope you're not expecting me to come and fetch you. I hate driving in the snow. The roads are so slippery and dangerous."

"Eddie, there have been multiple blizzards. The phone lines have only just been repaired. The roads here are closed in both directions, and, word has it, they won't open until after Christmas."

"You mean I'm going to have to spend Christmas in this hick little town all by myself? What am I supposed to do? Where will I go for Christmas dinner?"

"Eddie, this is no picnic for me either. Do you think I wanted this to happen? This was supposed to be a romantic getaway for us, our first Christmas together — the first of many Christmases together."

"Did you tell Richard you want a divorce?"

"No," she said quietly. "I thought long and hard about it. Richard will be heartbroken. He would have a terrible Christmas and so would the girls. Remember, they're so young — only 12 and 13. They'll be devastated. I couldn't do that to them, so I decided I would wait until I got back home to do it."

"Damn it! You always have an excuse, Marilyn. Sometimes, I have to wonder how serious you are about this relationship."

There was a knock. "There's someone at the door. It's probably the doctor coming to check on me. I'll call you later." She hung up. "Come in," she shouted.

Gabriel entered the room. "Aren't these beautiful?" She was carrying an enormous arrangement of flowers and placed them on the small coffee table. "Here you are, my dear." She handed Marilyn the card. "They were just delivered from Blooms and Baubles, the town florist next door. Anything I can get you?"

Marilyn shook her head. "No, thank you. You're right though. The arrangement is absolutely stunning." She held the card in her hand as she admired the tall, elegant-looking birds of paradise, striking stems of flaming-red ginger and white anthuriums surrounded by bright green branches of fir.

"Then I'll leave you to rest, and, hopefully, we'll see you in the dining room for dinner," Gabriel said as she left the room.

Marilyn read the card. It said, "I miss you. All my love — Richard." She thought for a moment, as she looked out the window at the plaza and considered the solitude. *Eddie didn't even ask how I was.* The tears welled in her eyes. She reached for her purse and pulled out a tissue.

CHAPTER 6

Cassie made her way to the dining room and was disappointed to see the notice that the restaurant wouldn't be open until 5.00 p.m. She heard chattering voices emanating from the neighboring room and looked up to see a sign that read "Rudolph's Tavern." *Not sure I should be having any alcohol in my state,* she thought, but decided to venture in anyway. Pushing through the saloon-style swing doors, she observed a typical rustic bar setting with wooden chairs and tables. Two large deer heads adorned each of the four walls. The names of the fictional reindeer from the poem, *'Twas the Night Before Christmas* were carved out of wood, painted in red, and hung from the antlers. Twinkling Christmas lights draped the bar itself and a silent jukebox sat in one of the corners. The tavern was empty save the fellow passengers from the flight, who were all seated around one of the tables.

"Good to see you," Fran called with a welcoming smile. "Come and join us."

"Hey guys! What are you so happy about? I have a splitting headache. Besides, it looks like we're all stranded here for Christmas." Cassie looked at all the drinks scattered across the table. "Wow, should everyone be drinking? I have to assume that, like me, you're all on some kind of medication," she said, in a half-joking manner.

"But we're alive, thanks to our masterful captain here," Marilyn said to the pilot who sat next to her as she patted him on the shoulder. "That's reason enough to celebrate. We're fortunate we all survived with relatively minor injuries so far. You look like you're in pretty good shape."

"I guess so. I just have a mild concussion. Thank you, Captain — if my memory serves — McFitten." She looked at the middle-aged man sitting next to the pilot and recognized him as the one who protected her during the crash. "And a huge thank you to you, Sir. I think you had a huge hand in saving my life. I'm eternally grateful."

The man stood and beamed at her. "Just did what came naturally, Ma'am. The name's Derek," he said, revealing a deep southern drawl. He pulled back the empty chair next to him and beckoned for her to sit.

"You're way too modest, Sir," Cassie grinned. "I seem to recall, that as the helicopter began hurtling toward the Earth, you wrapped your arms around me."

Derek leaned back in his chair. "I protected you as I would have protected my own daughter, or any other human for that matter."

A young waitress sporting an elf outfit emerged from behind the bar and greeted Cassie with a smile. "Welcome to Rudolph's Tavern. Here's our special cocktail menu, all made with our own recipes. Drinks are on the house this evening. There's also my own special, Eve's Eggnog."

Cassie looked at the menu and chuckled when she saw the creative list of drinks — Dasher's Delight, Dancer's Dandelion Wine, Prancer's Port, Vixen's Velvet Vodka, Comet's Cherry Cream Liqueur, Cupid's Champagne, Donner's Dry Martini, and Blitzen's Brandy Blend. She couldn't resist. "I think I'll have a Cupid's Champagne," she said.

Gabriel entered the bar and rang a bell to get everyone's attention. "Good evening, everyone. Merry Christmas and Happy Hanukkah," she said, her face beaming. "My husband and I know you're tired and probably even feeling a little drowsy from your various medications, so we're opening up the dining room early. Please come and join us in the restaurant for a hearty holiday meal. Don't worry about your drinks — our bar waitress, Sarah, will bring them into the dining room, where we'll be serving a delightful, very mild and healthy glühwein with your meal."

Multiple expressions of thank you blended with the sound of moving chairs as they all rose to follow Gabriel into the dining room. Everyone chuckled and smiled upon seeing the green tablecloths, each one embroidered in red with the items mentioned in The Twelve Days of Christmas — except for the five golden rings which were embroidered in gold.

"Care to join me for dinner?" Derek asked Cassie, as he observed a small booth for two.

"Sure," she replied, and he guided her to the table with the two turtle doves tablecloth.

Once seated, Cassie picked up the conversation where they left off. "Well, I'm not sure my father would have protected me the same way you did," she scoffed.

"Oh? Why do you say that?"

She toyed with her pendant. "I don't have a good relationship with my dad. We haven't spoken for years."

He suddenly took on a very paternalistic tone. "Well, I haven't spoken to my daughter in years either, but that doesn't mean I wouldn't protect her or be there for her if needed."

"My dad was overprotective. When I was growing up, he was so strict about who I dated, gave all the boys the third degree — it was embarrassing. He always said I wore too much makeup and my skirts were too short. 'You look so cheap,'" she said, mimicking her father.

"Sounds just like me. I said the same things to my daughter."

"Bet you didn't tell her she looked like a hooker or a prostitute."

Derek shook his head. "No. I guess I didn't call her that, but there were times when I could have. Maybe you'll understand one day when you have teenage children of your own."

Cassie laughed. "Now you're beginning to sound just like my father."

"Well, you can say what you like, young lady. But for all your father's strict admonitions, look how you've turned out. You're a smart, attractive young woman. You appear to have your head screwed on. Don't you think you owe at least some of that to your dad?"

Cassie thought for a minute. "I suppose so. I never quite looked at it that way." She felt momentarily uncomfortable and decided to turn the tables. "That's enough about me. Since you've given me an objective opinion from a parent's point of view, let's see if I can give you the perspective of a teenager. What's the deal with your daughter?"

"Rachel?" He shook his head again. "She turned out to be one huge disappointment. She's beautiful, talented, super smart. She could have been a straight "A" student if she had applied herself. I paid for her to take lessons in piano, ballet, horse riding, acting, you name it. We vacationed together in Europe. She had everything, and she excelled at everything. It was important to her."

"Important to you or to Rachel?" Cassie interrupted.

He was taken aback at the comment. "Well, for both of us, I suppose."

"Where was her mother during all this? You haven't mentioned her at all."

"She found someone else. We divorced, and she emigrated to Australia. Rachel receives a gift from her on her birthday and Christmas, as far as I know. At least, she was when we were still talking."

"What's Rachel doing now?"

"She married her high school sweetheart. He's an OK guy, I guess, but lacks ambition."

Now it was Cassie's turn to shake her head. "Well, let me tell you, something, Derek. If I was your teenage daughter and my mother walked out on me, I'd be blaming myself, wondering what I had done. I'd also try beyond belief to live up to your expectations so that both parents didn't desert me. I probably would have hated piano and ballet and all the rest of that stuff. Sure as heck could have done without those trips to Europe. The thoughts of whether or not you were going to drop me off at one of those prestigious finishing schools, where all parents seem to want to dump their kids, would have just terrified me. The school vacations would have been better at home, since it was the only security I had."

Derek was surprised by her candor.

Cassie continued. "Did you ever suggest counselling?"

"Of course not. I was her father. It was my responsibility to handle that."

"Now, you really could be my father." She smiled. "Exactly the same stance he adopted. If we had both gone to joint counselling, I'm convinced we'd be in a better position than where we are now."

"It wouldn't have worked. Rachel is far too smart and manipulative. She would have seen right through the counselor."

Cassie was exasperated. "But you didn't give her the benefit of the doubt. Don't you see? As a last resort, it may well have made a difference." She paused. "It certainly would have in my situation. I just know it," she said softly, then took a sip of her drink.

The door from the kitchen opened and Gabriel entered, followed by her portly husband, Mark. They were both carrying trays of soup. "Tonight, we are serving a mock turtle soup followed by roasted venison," Gabriel said in her warm, chirpy voice as they placed a bowl in front of each of the guests. "The venison will be served with roasted chestnuts, wild mushrooms, and butternut squash," Mark added. He had a cherubic face — a consummate maître d'.

Sarah entered the room holding a basket of bread rolls, which she started dispensing with wooden tongs. "I'll be bringing your glühwein, and tonight's dessert is a real treat — you'll be savoring my mother's homemade fruitcake," she said in cheerful tone.

"Before any of you groan," Mark chuckled, "Gabriel's fruitcake isn't your typical fruitcake. This one is made with loganberries, boysenberries, raspberries, mulberries, and all kinds of other berries."

Gabriel placed her empty tray on the nearby table. "And, those of you celebrating Hanukkah can enjoy my own homemade mandel bread."

The guests were speechless. Finally, Fran spoke up. "The dinner sounds absolutely heavenly. But, how are we going to repay you for all your kindness and hospitality?"

Mark put his arms around his wife and daughter. "There is no repayment," he said. "All you need to do is take time to heal. We want you to leave our village in a happier frame of mind than when you arrived here."

"And, you will," Gabriel beamed. "Merry Christmas and Happy Hanukkah!" As the hosts turned to leave, the captain called out.

"Wait a minute," he said. "I had one more passenger who was on the flight. Where is he?" Noticing there was no one else in the dining room, save the passengers from the flight, he continued, "And, by the way, where are the other guests?"

"The missing passenger. Ah, yes. That would be Oscar," said Gabriel. "He has a fractured leg, so we had him transported to our veteran's home. Father Matthew oversees the facility, and he'll make sure that Oscar receives all the care he needs. They don't call it the Heavenly Home for Disabled Veterans for nothing. As for the other guests, there are none. We close every year for the week of Christmas. We believe most people want to spend their holidays at home with their families and loved ones."

"Now, please everyone," Mark interjected. "*Bon Appetit.* Enjoy your dinner. Tomorrow is Christmas Eve, and the local townsfolk will stage a production of "A Christmas Carol" at the town hall. It's an annual tradition here. The performance is followed by a potluck dinner and caroling before winding down with an evening service by Father Matthew from the veterans home. You're all invited to attend. Like most potlucks, there is always plenty of food," he chuckled. "You just need to bring yourselves. The play starts at 6.30 p.m. It will probably seem very amateurish and provincial by your standards, but we always enjoy it. If you exit the hotel, make a right. When you get to the end of Poinsettia Plaza, make a left, and the town hall will be on your right. It will be so well lit you won't miss it. If you don't feel up to the walk in the crisp night air, Gabriel and I will be happy to drive you." He pointed to the entrance of the dining room. "And now, to help with your dining pleasure, the pure sounds of our local Dickensian singing quartet, Carole's Carolers, who have requested to come sing for you. We're sure you'll appreciate the harmonizing of our soprano, alto, tenor, and bass. By the way, they will be leading the caroling tomorrow evening, so tonight is just a little preview." He smiled and left the room.

The guests turned to face the dining room entrance and saw the two female singers clad in red, velvet Victorian dresses with matching bonnets, while their male counterparts were dressed in dark-green velvet suits with matching top hats. The quartet immediately began singing in perfect harmony, "God rest ye merry gentlemen, let nothing you dismay."

CHAPTER 7

The next morning, the sun was shining high in the clear blue sky, and even though her fractured shoulder was still giving her pain, Fran wrapped herself up warmly and decided to take a walk. It was time to pay a visit to The Gingerbread House to thank the Hollyberrys for their generous gift.

Oh, what a beautiful crisp morning — the air is so fresh, I can almost feel Jack Frost nipping at my nose. She treaded carefully around the snow where possible as she made her way across Poinsettia Plaza and marveled at the brightness of the red blooms themselves. *It's all so still — so quiet, peaceful, and serene.* She headed toward the giant Christmas tree in the center of the square, hearing only the sound of her own footsteps. *Wow, you sure can't beat the smell of a fresh pine tree at Christmas. It definitely makes the season festive.*

Enjoying the tranquility of the moment, Fran sat on one of the four benches surrounding the tree, nursing her arm. *The size of all those baubles is incredible! And, how in the world have they stayed there? I can't believe the wind from the storms hasn't sent them crashing to the ground. Strange. And, where are all the cars?* She looked around the square and saw the parking meters neatly spaced from each other in a symmetric pattern with no cars parked in the bays. *It's obvious the town doesn't rake in cash from parking fees.* Fran smiled. It was getting chilly, so she decided it was time to move on.

Fran turned on Candy Cane Lane, remembering Noel's directions. *Third shop down on the right-hand side.* She stopped at the corner to look in the window of The Entertainment Elves. Her eyes lit up with nostalgia as she scanned the merchandise. They had holiday albums for sale by the Carpenter's, Johnny Mathis, Andy Williams, Mannheim Steamroller, and other well-known artists. To the right of those, her favorite Christmas DVDs were prominently displayed: "*White Christmas*," "National Lampoon's Christmas Vacation," "It's A Wonderful Life," and several versions of "Miracle on 34th Street." Sprinkled in between were the works of famous authors, including Charles Dickens, O Henry, and Harriet Beecher Stowe. Fran was surprised to see the names of Tolstoy and Louisa May Alcott on a couple of the books, unaware either author had ever written a Christmas story. *There's not a single item in here that isn't holiday themed.* She wondered how they could survive all year long. *I guess Christmas is more of a lifestyle than a season for the people who live here — part of their culture, their DNA.*

The next store was Yule Love It Linens, and Fran recognized a replica of her hotel bed duvet hanging in the window. When she finally arrived at The Gingerbread House, the wonderful aroma of freshly baked cookies greeted her, beckoning her inside. Noel was behind the counter. Upon seeing her, he beamed and rushed to give her a hug.

"Be careful," she cried. "My arm's still in a sling, and it's very, very painful."

He ignored her remark, grabbed her by the hand, and guided her through the store, zigzagging between the scattered ice cream tables. "Mum, Dad, this is the nice lady I was telling you about," he hollered, as they ran through the kitchen doors. "This is Fran."

Fran blushed. She ruffled her hands through Noel's tousled hair and smiled at the Hollyberrys, whose faces were covered in flour from the dough they were tirelessly kneading. "You've done a fine job of raising this young boy. He's so well-mannered and loveable. But, that's not what I came to tell you," she said. "I wanted to thank you for such a thoughtful gesture yesterday. The cookies were absolutely delicious, and they really brightened my day, as I'm sure they did for the rest of the survivors too."

A petite but very pregnant Mrs. Hollyberry stopped what she was doing, wiped her hands on her apron, and walked Fran back to the front of the store. "Noel told us all about you," she said. "I wish you hadn't gone to the trouble of coming all this way when your arm must be in pain. Why don't you stay for a while?" she asked and pointed to one of the tables. "Have a cup of coffee or a latte — on the house, of course."

Fran thought for a moment. "All right, I don't mind if I do. A latte would be lovely, thank you. And, actually, I'm glad I came. I took a stroll through the town square to get here."

"Ah, yes," Mrs. Hollyberry said. "It sure is beautiful."

"So pretty," Fran agreed. "And so peaceful."

"Noel, would you be a dear and make your friend here a latte?" As he turned to walk away, his mother stopped him. "Warm up one of our mincemeat tarts for her too."

"So, do you know how long you will be staying in our village?" she asked, turning her attention back to her guest.

Fran shook her head. "No. It looks like we'll be here through Christmas. I guess another storm is coming, and they can't clear the roads."

Noel hollered again from behind the counter. "Can't she come and have Christmas dinner with us? Her son would also have been ten years old on Christmas Day, but he died."

Fran was embarrassed and sorry that Noel had shared what she assumed would be a secret between them. *Well, he's just a kid, I suppose. Can't blame him for blurting out what pops into his mind.*

"Well, of course, she can join us. That's if she doesn't mind spending it with just the three of us. Maybe she'd prefer to spend it with her friends at the hotel."

"Oh, I couldn't impose," Fran responded hastily. "Honestly, I couldn't. You have enough mouths to feed."

Noel brought the latte and tart over to the table. "Oh, please join us, Fran. It would be a nice birthday present for me. Please," he pleaded, tugging at her left arm again.

Mrs. Hollyberry laughed. "She won't if you keep grabbing her left arm. Now, let go of it, and see if you can help your papa with the baking." She could tell he was pouting, just by the way he put his hands in his pockets, and scuffled into the kitchen. "Seriously, we'd love to have you join us. You've made such an impression on Noel."

Fran shrugged. "He's a sweet young boy. Not sure what I said or did that was so impressionable."

Mrs. Hollyberry reached across the table, and clasped her hand. "I am so sorry for your loss. I can't imagine the pain you went through."

Fran managed a wan smile. "Thank you. It wasn't easy. It still isn't, actually, especially at this time of the year." Not wanting to dwell on the subject, she switched gears. "So … when's your due date, Mrs. Hollyberry?"

"Early February. It's going to be a boy. And, please, call me Ruth. We start dinner around three on Christmas Day. We do cake and ice cream for Noel's birthday afterwards, and, then, we take him to the outdoor ice rink because he loves to skate. You wouldn't want to disappoint the boy on his birthday by not showing up, would you? His siblings are in California visiting my sister and brother-in-law. They wanted to go to Disneyland."

"Well, if that's the case, I'd love to join you. Thank you."

"I'll have my husband, Solomon, pick you up at the inn around two."

Fran wondered why Noel didn't join his siblings. As if reading her mind, Noel reappeared. "Hey, are you going to the town hall for the show tonight? I'm playing the part of Tiny Tim. I get to say the line 'God Bless us Everyone.' It's the first time I've been asked to play the role."

Ruth chuckled. "The play is kind of fun. The gentleman who plays Scrooge has been doing it for the last three years. Oddly enough, his name is Luke Cratchit. He owns Cratchit's Crafts down the way on Mistletoe Mews. He should probably be playing the part of Bob Cratchit. Noel's so excited to be playing Tiny Tim. He's put his heart and soul into the role. We were all going to California this Christmas, but since this will be our last one with Noel, we acquiesced to his wishes. Playing the role of Tiny Tim was more important to him than seeing Jiminy Cricket, his favorite Disney character. Unfortunately, the other kids had their hearts set on going to Disneyland, and we couldn't disappoint them. So, we're having a split family holiday this year."

"That's going to be tough for you, isn't it?"

"Yes. But my sister and family were all here for Thanksgiving, so we made it a combined Christmas. That's why it will be extra nice for you to be here tomorrow — and at the play tonight."

Fran smiled and sipped her latte. "Well, how can I say no to an invite like that?"

CHAPTER 8

Fran didn't want to overstay her welcome, so she thanked Ruth and said goodbye before wandering further down the street to explore the rest of the charming village and buy some gifts to take to her hosts on Christmas Day. She paused at an imposing, multi-storey log building to read the sign, Heavenly Home for Disabled Veterans. She decided to stop in and say hi to her fellow passenger. *Not that it will make much difference,* she thought. *He seemed like a real curmudgeon. But, who knows, maybe the accident changed his heart.*

The warm and friendly Father Matthew greeted Fran and directed her to the porch at the rear of the building. "You'll find Oscar resting out back. He wanted some fresh air. If the opportunity presents itself, try and convince him to stay with us after he is healed. We could certainly use him here. I have talked to him about it, but I'm afraid I'm not having much success." Recognizing the confused look on Fran's face, he continued, "Oscar could be a great mentor to our vets suffering for post-traumatic stress disorder. Many of our residents are continually grappling with the condition." Fran wondered if Oscar might also be suffering from it but kept her thoughts to herself.

"I'll see what I can do," she smiled. "Not making any promises though."

When she saw Oscar, she couldn't help but feel sorry for him. His leg was in a cast, outstretched on the chaise lounge with his crutches on the floor next to him. Wondering if he would even recognize her, she extended her hand and introduced herself.

"Of course, I remember you," Oscar replied. "One of the passengers from the helicopter. Looks like you didn't fare too well either," he said, noting her arm in the sling.

Fran chuckled. "Well, by the looks of it, I'm certainly doing better than you. Anyway, I was in the area and thought I would pop in to see how you were doing."

"Just in the area? How did you happen to be 'just in the area?'"

"Oh, the local bakery, a shop called The Gingerbread House is literally around the corner. Yesterday, they sent me and the rest of the survivors a basket of delicious goodies, so I stopped by to thank them. It's such a picturesque little town, I decided to walk around for a bit, and lo and behold, here I am."

"A young boy delivered a basket to me, too. It was a nice gesture. I'll have to try and send them a thank you note, since I don't have the luxury of walking around the corner," he grumbled.

"Now, now, this is not the time for self-pity. It's Christmas! We have to make the best of our situation. Looks like you're not doing too badly here. Seems as if this is a nice place, and look at this beautiful garden of fresh vegetables." She cast her eyes on the tomato vines along one of the garden walls, the stalks of corn with multiple ears against another, and beanstalks along the third. The vegetable beds in front of her displayed healthy-looking cabbage, pumpkins, lettuce, and potatoes. She even noticed a few carrots protruding from the soil, showing off their distinct color and bushy tops. "This looks like a beautiful painting. How in the world do all of these veggies survive at this time of the year in the freezing cold? Why aren't they all covered in snow?"

Oscar shrugged. "Who knows? Everything seems very strange here."

The words struck a chord with Fran. She remembered marveling at the perfectly shaped Christmas Tree in Poinsettia Plaza, the large baubles that were somehow able to withstand the windy storms, and the poinsettias totally devoid of snow.

"They do have residents here who take care of the garden though," Oscar mentioned. "I will say, the food here is great. How are things where you are? And, how are the other passengers from the flight? Father Matthew told me there were no fatalities, but that's all I know."

"That's right. Everyone suffered injuries in varying degrees. But we're all OK. Too bad you can't be with us."

"Well, in a few days, all of you will probably be heading to wherever it was you were going before the crash. I'm going to be stuck here for a while, although Dr. Shepherd visited and said he is pleased with my progress. Hey, you don't happen to have a cigarette on you, do you? We can't smoke inside the building, but I guess we can smoke outside."

"Sorry, I don't smoke, but I'll see if I can find a store that sells cigarettes and get you some. Any particular brand?"

"That's so kind of you. Anything you can get your hands on will be fine. At this stage, I'll take anything, even a half-finished stogie," he chuckled. "My wallet is in the drawer next to my bed. Perhaps Father

Matthew will get it for you. Just take a few bucks out. I need something to occupy my time here."

Fran seized the opportunity. "I'm sure there are many ways you can put your time to valuable use in a place like this."

He stared at her for the first time. "I see Father Matthew wasted no time getting to you. Did he tell you he wants me to become a mentor?"

Seeing the annoyed expression on Oscar's face, she deftly sidestepped the question. "Well, it's something to consider," she said before changing the subject to family and where he lived. They chatted, albeit stiltedly, for another half-hour before Fran decided it was time to leave.

"Let me see about getting you those cigarettes."

Oscar stretched out his hand for hers. "Thank you."

She smiled. "It's the least I can do to thank you for your service to our country."

Fran found Father Matthew. As he handed her the cash for cigarettes, he told her about an old-fashioned dime store. "It's called Pennies from Heaven — it's a great little family-owned shop that's been here for years. It's on the corner at the end of this street, same side. You can't miss it."

"Thank you," she replied. "I'm looking forward to hearing your Christmas message tonight, Father. Will you be able to bring Oscar in his condition?"

"He doesn't know it yet, but he'll be there. The evening is billed as a potluck dinner, but, typically, Gabriel and Mark provide the meat, the Hollyberrys bring the desserts, and we cook up the vegetables. Our team of vets are in the kitchen preparing the veggies as we speak. They'll also be doing a lot of the serving tonight. Everyone here goes. Oscar will be no exception."

Fran smiled and turned to leave.

"God bless you, my child," the Father said.

She waved. "He already has."

CHAPTER 9

Cassie stood in the hotel lobby staring at the menu, debating if she could afford to have lunch in the café or whether she should venture into the town to see what other options there were. The headaches, which she assumed were a result of her concussion, were excruciating. Luckily, she didn't have to think too hard since the decision was made for her.

"Fancy running in to you here. Care to join me for lunch?"

Cassie turned to see Derek standing behind her. She smiled at him. "Good morning. I was just deciding whether to eat here or explore the town."

"We can eat here if you'd like. My treat. Fractured ribs make it too painful to do much walking. Besides, our hosts have been so gracious and hospitable, I thought the least I could do is support their restaurants. Come on."

Cassie hesitated.

"I'd sure appreciate the company," Derek persisted.

Now that he mentioned it, I could use some company too. "Well, OK — if you insist."

"I do insist," he said, as he gently steered her to a nearby table and pulled out a chair for her.

They grumbled about their aches and pains for a few moments before turning their attention to the "Anytime Menu." Cassie laughed out loud as she read some of the items. "Fancy having a Comet's omelet with Dasher's rashers of bacon or Cupid's cucumber and crab salad," she said.

Derek was equally amused. "How about Vixen's venison patties or Blitzen's bangers in a blanket."

Cassie placed her finger to her lip, as if in deliberation. "Actually, I'm looking for something sweet this morning. Maybe I'll try Donner's donuts or Dancer's Danish pastries. Although ... Prancer's pancakes look pretty tempting."

Sarah, the waitress from the night before, appeared with water and to take their orders.

"What exactly is Scrooge's scramble?" asked Derek.

"Oh, it's scrambled eggs with small chunks of bison, beef and wild boar," said Sarah cheerfully.

"Sounds delightful — that's what I'll have."

"And, I'll take a full order of Marley's maple waffles."

"Would you like some coffee or hot holiday cocoa to go with that?" Sarah asked. They both chose the cocoa served with marshmallows and cinnamon.

"Are you going to the play tonight?" inquired Derek.

"Sure. Believe it or not, I've never actually seen a version of the stage play. My dad wasn't big on those things. Sounds like it could be fun." Cassie shrugged. "At least it's something to do. How about you?"

"Well, I never took my daughter to see the play when she was a child either. I learned a lot from our conversation last night. I have a lot of making up to do. Thanks for showing me the way. I owe you a huge debt of gratitude."

"On the contrary, Derek. It is I who should be thanking you. I can't believe how selfish I was growing up, and how hard it had to be for my dad. I, too, spent much of last night reflecting on our conversation. It took a lot of soul-searching, and it was hard, but you've given me a new perspective. I hope my dad and I can get back on track and that he can forgive me."

"I'm sure he will. Surely, you can forgive each other? I know that is what I'm hoping from my daughter."

*****

Marilyn was enjoying her hot cup of coffee on the enclosed patio of the hotel. She felt the Christmas spirit as she looked out at Poinsettia Plaza through the glass. She was tempted to go for a stroll but was concerned it might exacerbate the pain in her back. She was enjoying the peace and solitude when her cellphone rang and startled her, making her jump.

"Richard, it's so good to hear your voice."

"I miss you, sweetheart. I wish I could be there with you, to put my arms around you and tell you how much I love you."

Marilyn laughed. "Then, I'm glad you're not here. I don't think my bruised body could take any hugging right now."

"Well, take the hugs in spirit, anyway. I've been checking the weather forecast and monitoring the road conditions. Looks like there are still snow storms happening *en route* to where you are, but they've cleared much of the road — just not enough to open them up by tomorrow. You'll be spending Christmas alone. I hate that."

"It's not so bad. Last night, we had an early holiday meal and carolers even stopped by to sing to us. And, tonight our hosts have a whole list of festivities planned. We'll start at the town hall, where we'll be treated to a staging of "A Christmas Carol." That will be followed with a potluck dinner, Christmas caroling, and service by a local minister to wrap up the evening."

"What in the world are you taking to the potluck?"

"They told the survivors not to bring anything due to our condition."

"Sounds like you're really being taken care of."

"The people here have the most giving hearts. Generosity just comes naturally to them — it's who they are. And, I must say, it's very refreshing. How are things on the home front?"

"The same, sort of, but we miss you. It's so quiet. When you're not here, it feels like we're living in a house, a place to occupy. But you turn it into a loving home. Oh, gotta go. There's someone at the front door. I'll call you later."

She was relieved when he hung up — not only because she felt guilty talking to him but also because it meant she could call Eddie. He answered with a snappy tone.

"Why are you so grouchy?" she asked in disbelief.

"Maybe it has something to do with the fact that I'm at a grocery store, doing last-minute shopping so that I can cook myself dinner on Christmas Day and eat it alone. And did I mention the aisles are so jam-packed with rude people that I can barely move my cart? Plus, you know how much I hate shopping … and cooking."

"I can't believe you're so insensitive. I'm stuck by myself too … and with a lot of pain to boot. I don't even know when I will be able to leave here."

"It's your own fault. I told you not to get in that helicopter, but you insisted."

"Well, there are other places we could have met, but you're the one who insisted I come here to visit you at Christmas. And, the more we talk, the more I wonder what possessed me to say yes in the first place."

"And the more I'm wondering what possessed me to extend the invite."

Angrily, she hung up. She pulled a tissue from her purse and blotted her tear-filled eyes. *What a Christmas this is turning out to be.*

CHAPTER 10

"God bless us, everyone," grinned Noel, as he took center stage for the most memorable line of "A Christmas Carol."

Shortly afterwards, the lights came up in the town hall, and Fran, unable to applaud with her arm still in a sling signaled her approval with a thumbs up. The rest of the audience clapped enthusiastically. As soon as the applause stopped, Noel stepped down from the stage and ran to welcome Fran and her fellow travelers.

"Gee, thank you all for coming," he beamed. "And especially you, Sir," he continued, shaking Oscar's hand. "It can't be very comfortable sitting with your leg outstretched like that."

Oscar was seated at the end of the table, his leg raised on a cushioned stool. "The truth is, I hadn't planned on coming, but Father Matthew said I had to if I wanted something to eat for dinner. No one would have been at the home to serve it, since everyone was here watching you." He winked and smiled at the boy.

That's the first time I've seen that man crack a smile. I can't believe it ... and, then, on top of that, he winked? thought Fran.

"Well, you won't have to wait for your meal here," Noel said excitedly. "I'm helping out, and I'll make sure this table is served first."

Oscar grabbed his arm. "Before you dash off, you little bundle of energy, perhaps you could have your parents stop by our table? I'd like to personally thank them for the delicious cookies."

"Sure will, Mister." He disappeared into a room behind the raised rostrum that served as the stage.

The travelers chatted together and enthused about the play for a few minutes. "I didn't have a chance to see everything before the play," Marilyn said as she noticed the décor. "Look how festive it is in here." The others turned to see red and green linens draping the tables. From the matching napkins to the snow globe centerpieces, each of them noticed something worth pointing out. "Look at the beautiful tree in the corner — it's so pretty, it almost makes me forget about my back pains." She was trying to stay focused on the evening instead of on Eddie and what he was doing alone in Cody.

"Well, I guess we can thank Gabriel and Mark for reserving a table for us front and center. And, look at these!" Cassie said excitedly. Little porcelain Christmas trees that were hand-painted and decorated sat in front of each place setting. She picked one up and admired every last detail. "I wonder if they're ours to keep. If not, I hope I can buy one."

Noel returned with a trolley and started serving the attendees. "By the way, I couldn't help but to overhear you, and the trees are yours to keep. They're party favors, courtesy of Mr. Cratchit, owner of Cratchit's Crafts. He played the part of Scrooge in tonight's play. He makes a gift every year for everyone who comes — he's kind and generous."

Marilyn held up the ornament in the center of the table and appreciated the delicacy of the artwork. "There seems to be an abundance of people like that in this community," she said. "And, looking around this room, there has to be at least 250 people here." The others nodded in agreement as they took their first few bites of what could possibly be the best Christmas dinner they'd ever had. Several locals stopped by the table to welcome the travelers and offer help if needed. The room was filled with the sounds of laughter bouncing off the walls and the air felt as if it were wrapping everyone in a warm embrace.

Toward the end of the meal, Carole's Carolers entered the hall, dressed in the same Victorian costumes as the night before and made their way to the center of the stage. The tenor, Johannes, adjusted his hat slightly. "Good evening and Merry Christmas," he said. "It's Christmas Eve, and that can only mean one thing: Our lovely soprano, Carole, will start the evening with a solo of 'Ave Maria.' Our alto, Hannah, will follow with 'Oh Holy Night.' Afterwards, we will hand out song sheets so you can all join us in singing some Christmas carols before Father Matthew delivers his annual Christmas message." Carole started singing a cappella, and the room fell totally silent to make way for the crystal-clear dulcet tones of Franz Shubert's famous song as they pervaded the hall. Thunderous applause erupted when she finished, but Hannah had no problem following her and received an equal amount of enthusiasm when she sang the final notes of her hymn.

As many of the veterans cleared away the paper plates, others delivered cookies, cider, and song sheets to each table.

How amazingly harmonious everyone sounds, thought Derek, who had always hoped his daughter would develop an interest in music. *This is turning into such a beautiful evening. I almost feel guilty for being thankful that we had the accident. These last two days have been a life-altering experience for me.*

After several carols had been sung, Johannes stepped forward. "Before we call it a night and turn it over to Father Matthew, give yourself a big hand for being a great audience." The sound of applause quickly took over. "We have one more song. It's our closing carol, 'Silent Night.' Could someone please switch off the light?" The room went dark except for the twinkling lights on the tree and those on the stage.

A serene atmosphere emanated through the hall as the carolers sang with an unexpected softness. As Fran looked sideways, she saw snowflakes falling ever so softly outside the window. *How peaceful.*

Father Matthew finally took to the stage, thanking the carolers and everyone else who made the evening possible. "As you know, each year, I wish each and every one you three gifts. We are reminded that the wise men arrived in Bethlehem bearing the gifts of gold, frankincense, and myrrh. Last year I asked you to receive the gifts of faith, hope, and charity. This year, I am offering you peace, love, and joy. Simply put, may each and every one of you here find peace. Not only peace for the world, but for peace of mind. May you find love in your hearts and discover the joy of giving … especially giving of oneself."

As he continued with his sermon, elaborating on his three gifts, the messages were not lost on those who, either by divine intervention or a twist of fate, had found themselves stranded in this village at Christmastime.

CHAPTER 11

I t was Christmas morning.

Oscar woke up and saw a neatly made, empty bed across from his. *Andrew is probably helping cook breakfast,* he thought, wondering why his roommate was not there to help him out of bed. Lying there, he pondered his situation. There was a soft knock on the door, and Father Matthew, dressed in his customary clerical attire, entered.

"Good morning, and a Merry Christmas to you, Oscar," he said and smiled. "Have a good night's sleep? And how's that leg of yours feeling today? Need some help getting up and onto the crutches?" He pulled back the drapes.

"Merry Christmas to you, too, Father," Oscar replied. "Leg's feeling a little better, thank you. But, no, I had a terrible night's sleep. And it's all your fault."

The minister was taken aback. "Oh, and how's that?"

Oscar grinned at him. "You gave me a lot to think about with your sermon last night, Father. I suspect you gave a lot of people pause to reflect."

"Well, I'm pleased you found my talk beneficial." Knowing how Oscar felt about religion, he was curious as to what had moved the veteran.

As if reading his mind, Oscar pulled himself up in bed and continued. "It was the three gifts that you spoke of — joy, peace, and giving. When I got into bed last night, I couldn't remember the last time I'd had such an enjoyable evening. All of the people in this village giving so much of themselves, so joyously and with so much love in their hearts. I started thinking about the days since I've been here. You've given me a place to recuperate. Everyone here has helped me in and out of chairs. Andrew, my roommate, has been a saint. Dr. Shepherd is here constantly to check on me. And, I've enjoyed so many great meals. The first day I was here, that kid who was in the play last night brought a basket of cookies from his parent's bakery store. I understand they also provided the pumpkin pies for last night."

Father Matthew listened intently as Oscar resumed his tribute. "And speaking of last night, look at the meals provided for all of those people by you and the owners of the inn, the carolers singing for free, and the store owner who made all those party favors

— such a kind gesture." He paused again, and shook his head in disbelief. "While I was eating, there seemed to be so much joy and happiness. So much laughter in the room." He shrugged. "Everyone pitched in to make it so. Me and the rest of the survivors were treated like royalty. It seems as if no one here has a care in the world."

"I'm sure most of them do have cares and worries," interjected Father Matthew. "They just love and help others where they can, which gives them their peace of mind."

"Well, Father, peace of mind is certainly something that's eluded me for the longest time. I'm not sure I'll ever find that."

"Whatever it is that's so burdensome, you can surely confide in me."

"You want me to participate in a confessional?"

"Not really. Just talk like one human being to another. If, as you say, you'll go on your merry way after your leg is better, no one will ever know, and at least you will have gotten whatever is troubling you off your chest." He sat down on Andrew's bed and clasped his hands together, an earnest expression on his face.

Oscar turned his head away and stared out of the window. "I thought I had peace of mind, Father. But then I went to serve my country during the Vietnam War. It was hell …sheer hell. I thought we'd all be there forever. As good fortune would have it, I had the best of buddies. His name was Jack. We were the same age. Ironically, he was from a little town in Minnesota called Peace Township. He was married with two young kids — a girl and a boy. We had each other's backs. He was there for me when I needed him, which was often. One day, we were in a remote town north of Saigon. It had been raining. There was mud everywhere. The humidity was terrible. We were sweating like pigs." Oscar paused for a short while, as if in contemplation.

"As the sun started to set, the town with its primitive huts was ambushed. It was obvious we were extremely outnumbered. In no way could we have fought off the enemy. The sound of gunshots and children and women screaming rang loudly in my ears. It still does. Jack and I started to head for the jungle even though we knew the enemy would follow us. I was a faster runner than Jack, so I was ahead of him. Suddenly, I heard him yell out, 'Ozzie, help me!' That's what he called me — Ozzie. I looked back. Jack had tripped over a rock or something. He was lying in a pool of mud, his backpack still strapped to him. His arm reached out toward me, motioning for help. I could see the look of pain and fear in his muddied face, but I couldn't go back and save him.

STEPHEN MURRAY | 77

The voices of the enemy were loud. They would have captured and tortured both of us. Probably killed us."

He turned to face the minister. "So, you see, Father Matthew. I doubt I will ever have peace of mind. I wasn't there for my best buddy. His face, filled with terror, haunts me to this day. And you know what? When I returned home, I received a letter from his wife, asking me what I knew about Jack. I couldn't reply. I didn't know what to say." He stopped and scratched his forehead. "I've never told this to anyone. I have no idea why I'm telling you." Oscar cast his head downward, as if in shame.

Silence fell between the two gentlemen.

The door opened, and Andrew entered. "Sorry Father, I didn't know you were here. Breakfast will be ready soon. I thought I'd come and give Oscar a hand and help him to the dining room."

"Don't worry, I'll help Oscar. We'll be there in a few minutes."

Andrew nodded and closed the door.

The priest reached out and placed his hand gently on Oscar's shoulder.

"Well, Oscar, part of your healing process can at least begin now. You've opened up, which is the first step. As I mentioned before, I hope you'll consider staying here after your leg has recovered. Most of the veterans here served in Afghanistan and Iraq. We do have a couple of Vietnam vets, though, and one from the Korean War. As I told you before, many suffer from PTSD. They could certainly use someone to talk to — especially someone who has been through it. I think you'd be an asset. And, most importantly, I think that once you see how good it feels to give yourself to others, to help other people heal, you'll start to lighten the weight of the guilt you've been carrying around."

They looked at each other for a moment, and Oscar suddenly realized what just happened.

"Geez, I didn't mean to be a downer on Christmas, Father. I know it's a special celebration for you. When you came in, I wanted to have an upbeat conversation because of all the great things I experienced last night. Now I've ruined your day."

"On the contrary, you haven't, Oscar. It pleases me to no end that you've been able to verbalize your trauma. Please, just think about my suggestion. Now, let's get you up and to the bathroom to brush your teeth. Then, we'll get you to the dining room for a hearty Christmas breakfast." He helped Oscar out of bed and handed him his crutches.

Back to his grousing, Oscar gingerly asked, "If I considered staying what would I do to pass the time?"

"Oh, if you like fishing, you could help our two fishermen here catch fish for the group."

Oscar perked up. "There's fishing in these parts?"

"Sure, we have a great lake nearby. Nice thing is, we're exempt from the license and the number of fish we catch. We can get you a fishing pole and some tackle at the Anglers Angel, if that's something you enjoy."

"It's always been a hobby of mine."

Father Matthew was encouraged by the progress. "At breakfast, I'll introduce you to our resident fishermen. I'm sure they have lots of stories to tell about the one that got away."

They both laughed.

CHAPTER 12

"We have to stop meeting like this, Cassie. People are going to start a rumor soon."

"Derek, what a pleasant surprise. Merry Christmas! Will you join me for a nice cup of hot chocolate?" She was sitting in the enclosed porch but rose to give her new friend and mentor a hug.

"Now, *that* will start a scandal," he joked, wagging his finger at her. "Even so, I don't mind if I do join you for a hot chocolate," he added, noticing the steam emanating from her mug on the table and the delicious aroma. "And Merry Christmas to you too — aren't you looking festive?"

Cassie was clad in red boots, green pants and a cheery Santa sweater. "I thought it might raise my spirits out of the gloom I feel this Christmas. How sad is that?"

Derek sat down next to her and leaned back in his chair. "Well, the point is, did it work? I mean, dressing up festive. Did it cheer you up?"

Cassie shook her head, and toyed with her Christmas charm bracelet. "Believe it or not, I was actually looking forward to seeing my dad again and meeting his wife. He called me this morning. We had the best chat. I sensed he really was eager to see me too. But instead, I get to spend Christmas Day alone." She looked forlornly out the window as she placed her hands around the china mug that sported a partridge in a pear tree design.

"Well, it's a good step in the right direction that you were keen to see your dad. After all these years, I was anxious to see my daughter too. Though, at least Rachel called me this morning. Pity isn't it? Seems like both you and I have wasted so much time. Maybe this accident was meant to happen." He shrugged. "Perhaps we were both meant to have this reality check before meeting our families. Get a fresh perspective, if you will."

Cassie looked askance. "How did you get to be so philosophical and wise?"

"Age and experience, I suppose. But, I'm not as wise as you suggest. Otherwise, I wouldn't have allowed the estrangement between Rachel and me to fester for so long. Anyway, you won't be alone for the entire time today. I'll be here, as I'm sure will the others. We'll make the best of it."

Sarah arrived at the table. "Merry Christmas to you. May I get you anything?" Derek ordered hot chocolate with extra whipped cream. Having overheard Derek's remarks, Sarah continued, "Don't worry about being alone. We have a wonderful Christmas dinner prepared with all the trimmings. Every Christmas after dinner we take a sleigh ride down to the rink. The kids from school showcase a Nativity on ice. It's kind of cute. They put their hearts and souls into it. Then, they open the ice rink up for everyone to skate. The snow stopped early this morning, and it doesn't look as if we'll have any more today. Maybe you'll join us. You can rent skates there."

"Sounds like a great idea. I haven't skated in years. But, I'm not sure my fractured ribs and bruised spine would welcome a spin around the rink," Derek teased.

Sarah immediately felt a pang of guilt over her insensitivity. "Oops! Sorry. I forgot." She immediately disappeared into the kitchen.

"Gosh, skating takes me back," reminisced Cassie. "I haven't skated for a long time either, and not sure I will with my concussion, even though the diagnosis is mild. Skating can make a person dizzy in a real short time. But it sounds like fun to go and watch the kids perform the Nativity. And, the sleigh ride sounds magical. I wonder how far away it is?"

Sarah returned from the kitchen with the hot chocolate and placed the cup in front of Derek. His mug featured a motif of the two turtle doves. "Sorry, I couldn't help but overhear. The sleigh ride leaves from here, goes around Poinsettia Plaza, past the town hall, and down Candy Cane Lane — all the way until it turns into Snowflake Way. The skating rink is about a half-mile down. The sleigh ride will be about ten minutes. It doesn't take long. I'll check back later to see if you want anything to munch on before Christmas dinner, which we'll be serving around four o'clock." She left the two to enjoy their drinks and conversation.

Cassie was relieved. "Well, I guess Christmas Day won't be so bad after all, even if it isn't what I was hoping for when I got dressed this morning." She reached out, patted Derek's arm and smiled. "I am grateful to you, Derek, for giving me such a different perspective about my dad. It's helped more than you'll ever know."

Derek placed his hand over hers. "No more than you've helped me," he reassured her. "Your insights and opinions have been invaluable and will go a long way to healing the breach between Rachel and me."

They both paused and sipped their hot drinks while looking at the plaza in front of them. Cassie broke the silence. "You know what also touched me a lot was the minister's sermon last night. I was so moved by his three gifts of joy, peace, and giving. I don't know why."

"Maybe you could relate to it," Derek responded. "I know it gave me food for thought, for sure. As it happens, I enjoyed the entire evening — the play, the carols, the potluck. It was, well ... just so Christmassy."

Marilyn suddenly interrupted their conversation. "So glad to find someone here. Can I join you? I didn't plan on spending my Christmas Day in a hotel room alone this year."

Derek pulled a chair back and beckoned for her to sit. "Merry Christmas, Marilyn. You're absolutely welcome to join us! Do you want me to go inside and order you some hot chocolate?"

"Thank you, but I bumped into Sarah along the way and asked if she would bring me some. It should be here soon." Marilyn started rubbing her hands to keep warm. "Chocolate smells good."

"What a pretty neckerchief and how very fitting," Cassie said and smiled as she noticed the white silk scarf covered with green holly and ivy leaves. A smattering of the red berries on the holly exactly matched her red cashmere sweater. "Mark and Gabriel will be thrilled you are promoting their inn so appropriately."

Marilyn laughed. "Thank you. I brought it along specifically to wear on Christmas Day. No reason I shouldn't wear it just because I'm not spending the day as planned." She removed her dark glasses, revealing red rings around her eyes. Cassie was of a mind to say something but decided against it. Her instincts were correct.

It had not been a good morning for Marilyn. Her husband, Richard, and two daughters had called so early they woke her up. She thought it a poor choice of tunes to sing "We Wish You a Merry Christmas" to her. It clearly wouldn't be. She waited a couple of hours before contacting Eddie. She hoped that, by now, he had more of the Christmas spirit than he demonstrated the previous couple of days. Her hopes were in vain. She left a message for him on his voicemail and had yet to receive a call hours later.

Derek also sensed something was amiss with Marilyn but assumed she just missed being with her family. Like Cassie, he also chose not to comment, focusing instead on the positive. "Cassie and I were just discussing how much we enjoyed everything last night. How did you like it?"

Marilyn lit a cigarette. "Oh, it was absolutely wonderful! The play was charming. The little boy playing Tiny Tim who delivered our cookies the other day was so cute. He almost stole the show. The food was good — especially for a potluck." She smiled and chuckled for the first time that day. "I was touched by the minister's service and particularly by all the townsfolk who stopped by our table to welcome us."

For a while, the three of them got so lost in conversation that they forgot about what brought them there.

CHAPTER 13

As Fran was coming down the staircase, she heard the chatter of voices and decided to stop in and spread some Christmas cheer while waiting for the Hollyberrys to pick her up.

"Well, there you are," exclaimed Marilyn, stretching out her arms to greet Fran. "Merry Christmas! I was wondering if you would ever come down. Will you join us? We started with hot chocolate but have moved on to Gabriel's yummy fruit cake and the special Eve's eggnog."

Fran placed the sizeable carrier bag she was holding on the floor and hugged all three gently as best she could with her arm still in the sling. "I would, but I've been invited over to The Gingerbread House. Seems little Noel has taken a shine to me, and it's his birthday today. He's turning ten, and he wanted me to be there for his party." She didn't want to bring down everyone's spirits, so she refrained from mentioning that she had a son who, like Noel, would have been celebrating his tenth birthday too. "Mr. Hollyberry will be here in five minutes. He said he would pick me up at two."

Marilyn glanced at her watch. "Goodness, I can't believe that's the time." She looked at Derek and Cassie. "Do you realize we've been chatting here for almost three hours?"

Derek laughed. "Well, see how time flies when you're having fun. You should have joined us, Fran. And, come to think of it, I wonder where Captain McFitten is. He should come down and be here with us."

"Oh, I bumped into the captain when I came down earlier this morning for something to drink. He was pouring some coffee for himself at the same time. He said he was going to spend the day in his room watching TV. I think he still feels bad about the accident. As for me — well, I did a lot of meditating this morning. That minister's talk last night and the events of the past few days gave me a lot to think about. You know what I mean?"

The others nodded in unison. They all knew exactly what she meant.

"There's Mr. Hollyberry now. Hope you all manage to make the best of what's left of Christmas Day." She picked up her purse and the carrier bag containing some wrapped gifts before she headed out the front door. Noel, complete with a Santa hat, jumped out of the passenger side of the car to greet her. "Gentle with the hugs now, Noel. Happy birthday to you and Merry Christmas!"

Solomon climbed out of the driver's seat and opened the rear car door for her.

Noel took Fran's arm and helped her down the steps while taking hold of her carrier bag. "Wow, are these gifts for me?" His face lit up as he looked at the beautifully wrapped presents in the bag.

"Noel, have you forgotten your manners?" his father asked sternly before turning his attention to Fran. "So glad you're spending Christmas Day with us." They exchanged hugs.

It was a short ride back and Ruth was waiting at the door when they arrived and greeted Fran with a big hug.

Fran removed her scarf and coat as she entered the house. "It was so kind of you to invite me. The aroma from the kitchen is just heavenly. Oh my! Your Christmas tree looks so magical." She stood for a moment, admiring the twinkling lights, beautiful baubles, and icicles hanging from the tree. Then she basked in the warm, loving feeling that pervaded the home. Noel handed her the carrier bag, which she placed under the tree.

Ruth straightened one of the strings of lights. "We all have a hand in the tree. It's one of our Christmas traditions. We trimmed it this year before the children left for Disneyland."

Noel jumped up and down. "Can I open up the gifts in this bag?"

Solomon chastised his son again and Noel pouted.

"At least we should make sure our guest is settled first, don't you think?" his mother asked, gesturing Fran to the sofa, which was covered with Santa cushions in various shapes and sizes. "Perhaps she would like some hot chocolate, a glass of eggnog, or wine. Maybe some hot apple cider?"

"A glass of eggnog would be nice, thank you. My fellow passengers from the flight were drinking them at the inn before I left. I just fancied one."

Solomon departed to the kitchen to pour the eggnog. "Pour me one too, will you?" his wife asked. "And, be a dear and check the thermometer in the turkey while you're at it." She looked at Noel who was still trying to peer inside the bag of gifts. "You don't even know if the gifts are for you. Leave that bag alone."

Fran chuckled. "Actually, they're not all for you, Noel. Why don't you pass me the bag?" He anxiously grabbed it and handed it to Fran.

Solomon returned with a tray holding four glasses. "Turkey's looking fine, honey. I took it out of the oven to sit for a while." He handed one of the glasses to Noel. "Here's some pumpkin flavored eggnog for you son, minus the alcohol." He winked at Noel, and turned to Fran. "I hope it's OK. I sprinkled some nutmeg on top of yours. I guess I should have checked first."

"What kind of eggnog is it without nutmeg?" asked Fran, smiling.

"Cheers, everyone. Merry Christmas," said Ruth raising her glass. The four glasses clinked as they all toasted.

There was a brief pause while they savored the drinks. Fran broke the silence. "Is now an appropriate time for the gifts?"

The Hollyberrys nodded, knowing how excited Noel was. Fran delved into the bag and retrieved a gift for Ruth, one for Solomon, and two for Noel, leaving the birthday gift in the bag for later.

Noel ripped the wrapping off one of his gifts with reckless abandon. "Wow," he exclaimed, with apparent glee. "Oh boy! Two DVDs! The original version of "A Christmas Carol" and "Scrooge." Can we watch one of them now? Please?" he pleaded. "I want to see how the boys play Tiny Tim."

Both of his parents replied with a firm no. "You can watch them tomorrow when we don't have guests. Anyway, we'll be having Christmas dinner shortly. Now, be a good boy, and let us open our gifts before you open your second one. And what do you say to your friend?"

Noel got up from his futon and walked over to Fran. He gave her a gentle hug and kiss on the cheek. "Thank you," he said, and plopped down on the couch next to her.

Ruth opened her gift and was delighted to see three different colored onesies for her soon-to-be newborn son. "These are absolutely lovely," she gushed, holding them up one by one for all to see. "How thoughtful, but you really shouldn't have."

"After all the kindness you've shown me, not to mention my fellow passengers from the accident — it's the very least I could do. As I was making my way back from your bakery yesterday, I stumbled across Kringle's Cribs and Baby Goods Boutique. What a charming store. The owner, Peter, was so helpful."

"He's the best," said Solomon, unwrapping his gift. "He and his wife have been friends of ours for years. We're all members of the local chamber of commerce. Oh my, look at this," he exclaimed, holding up a book titled "Creative Cookie Recipes for all Occasions." The cover displayed cookie cutters for every holiday imaginable — hearts for Valentine's Day, shamrocks for St. Patrick's Day, flags for the Fourth of July, turkeys for Thanksgiving, stockings and trees for the Christmas season, and the Star of David for Hanukkah.

Fran gently put her arm around Noel, who had snuggled up next to her. "I hope you like it, Solomon. John, at the Entertaining Elves shop, said he knew you didn't have it already. It's a newly published book, and the first shipment only arrived last week. Some of the recipes look very creative. You might not use any of them, but perhaps they will give you some ideas, anyway."

Solomon was touched. "Your gift is most generous and very thoughtful."

"You really didn't have to buy us anything," added Ruth. "Your being here to help celebrate Noel's birthday is more than a gift." She was mindful this would be their last Christmas together.

Noel took his mother's comments as a cue. "My turn, my turn to open a gift," he yelled with glee. The adults laughed as they watched him, once again, rip the paper off the present. "Oh, how cool are these? Look, Mom and Dad." He held up two pairs of ice-skating soakers — one pair with a huskie pattern and the other with mountain bears. "Thank you, Fran. Thank you. You are coming to watch me ice skate tonight, aren't you? Please?"

"They're so cute. Where did you find those? And where in the world did you find time to do all this shopping?" Ruth asked.

Fran took the final sip from her eggnog. "It was easy. After I left yesterday, I visited Oscar, one of the passengers from our flight who has a broken leg and is at Father Matthew's Heavenly Home for Disabled Veterans. I took a stroll around the town, and stopped by Kringle's Cribs. As you know, right next door is Samson's Sporting Goods, which is where I found the soakers for Noel. I remembered you telling me he enjoys ice skating on Christmas night.

Noel repeated his plea for Fran to join them. "Please, it's my birthday!"

"Don't badger her, Noel. Take your gifts to your room, and wash your hands. It's time for dinner. And, don't lollygag." Noel left the room, and Ruth finished her drink. "I think the turkey's probably ready for carving now, dear."

"Is there anything I can do to help?" asked Fran.

"You can come and stir the gravy if you like." Ruth smiled as they all left for the kitchen. "What did you think of Father Matthew's sermon last night?" she asked.

Fran shook her head. "Well, he's quite amazing. I've been meditating over what he said all morning. He sure gave me a lot to think about."

"He always does," said Solomon, as he started to carve the turkey.

CHAPTER 14

"There you are," hollered Andrew, as he stumbled across Oscar, who was sitting by himself on the back patio. "I wondered where you were."

"Well, it's not like you had to go too far to find me," grumbled Oscar, as he coughed on his cigarette. "It's not as if we reside in the White House."

Andrew laughed. "No, you're right about that. I came to help you inside."

"It's not dinner time already, is it?"

"No, it's 'count our blessings' time." He reached to help Oscar off the chaise lounge.

Oscar rolled his eyes. "Do I have to?"

Andrew ignored the question. "Actually, you'll probably enjoy it. All the residents gather in the activities room. One by one, we count our blessings. It's a program Father Matthew put in place. We do it before dinner on Easter, Memorial Day, Independence

Day, Thanksgiving, and Christmas. This year, he added the Jewish Passover, New Year's Day, Yom Kippur, and Hanukkah. Don't be surprised if he adds Rosh Hashanah and the Chinese New Year for that matter." He laughed again.

Oscar, unable to find fault with his always upbeat roommate, managed a weak grin. "I guess my blessing this year will be having a chirpy roomie."

"Hey, buddy. Lighten up. You have more blessings than you probably realize."

They arrived at the recreation hall. All the seats around the edge of the room were occupied except for two, which Oscar assumed were for Andrew and himself. Father Matthew was seated at the one end of the room in front of a statue of the Virgin Mary. The walls, in dire need of a fresh coat of paint were dominated by large posters. Oscar recognized them as replicas of the nine scenes representing the Book of Genesis from Michelangelo's Sistine Chapel. Even Oscar sensed a spiritual feeling. It was the first time he had been together with all of his fellow residents at the same time. He glanced around and suddenly felt very humbled.

One of the younger residents had a prosthetic leg, while another was the bearer of a prosthetic arm. Benjamin, one of the fishermen he'd met earlier, had a patch over his right eye. There were visible scars on the faces and arms of more than just a few of them.

Once Oscar and Andrew were seated, Father Matthew, started the proceedings. "Since it is Christmas Day, I'm sure you've all counted your blessings and discovered that you have many. We all want to hear about everyone's blessings, but we also want to feast later on. So, here's how it goes … We'll go around the room until everyone has shared one of their blessings — no repeats. The floor is open for comments before moving on to the next person. If time permits, we'll have two or three rounds. Whoever wants to start, just raise your hand."

Thank goodness, thought Oscar. *I'll see what everyone else has to say before I volunteer.* His roommate's arm shot up.

"Go ahead, Andrew," the pastor said.

"I'm blessed because we have two great cooks here. I get to chow down on great meals."

Everyone laughed.

"That's not quite what I had in mind," said Father Matthew, his tone gentle but firm.

"I know," replied a chastened Andrew. "Since it's Christmas, I was just having some light-hearted fun. Father, I count the Heavenly Home for Disabled

Veterans, as a true blessing. It's been a safe haven for all of us. Honestly it has."

A chorus of "amens" dominated the room.

Daniel was seated to the left of Andrew. "And following that, I would say that I count you, Father Matthew, as a blessing to everyone. You're always here for all of us." Everyone applauded as a second round of "amens" burst forth.

The minister blushed. "I'm sure you have greater blessings than myself and the home."

"I'm blessed to be born and raised in America," came the comment from one of the veterans seated in the far corner, who Oscar had not yet met.

"And blessed to have served my country, even if I did lose my right arm," added another.

Benjamin nodded. "Yes, at least we came back alive. That sure is a blessing. Many of our fellow men weren't blessed the same way."

The residents had ceased raising their hands, but Father Matthew was pleased with the thoughtful outpourings from his residents. He allowed the conversation to continue freely.

Oscar was torn. His best friend did not return from Vietnam. He felt pangs of guilt, but was simultaneously humbled, since he should have been considering his safe return from Asia as a blessing. He looked up, not recognizing the veteran who started singing "I'm proud to be an American, where at least I know I'm free." The residents who were able, rose from their chairs, placed their hands over their hearts, and joined in the singing. More than a few of them had tears in their eyes.

Oscar looked across the room at Father Matthew, wondering if this had been a ploy, but the minister was heavily immersed in what was happening around him. *I doubt he'd be so devious,* Oscar thought.

Several more blessings came forth expressing fortune for family, fellowship, and faith. Father Matthew was encouraged by the spontaneity of his flock and the complete involvement. As it transpired, there was only time for one blessing from each of those assembled — the vets relayed stories of their loved ones, experiences during their time of service, and the camaraderie. The minister looked at his watch. "OK. Time's up guys. Let's head to the dining room."

"Hey, not so fast, Father," said Andrew. "We still haven't heard from our new resident, Oscar." He nudged his roomie in the ribs.

The room fell quiet. All eyes focused on Oscar.

After a few moments of silence, Oscar looked around the room and took a deep breath. "Well, I must confess, I suppose I do have many blessings, some of which have already been mentioned. But one experience I doubt has befallen any of you. As you all know, there was a helicopter crash near here a couple of days ago. For as many times as I could have been killed in Vietnam, I could just as easily have died in the plane crash. Yet, all of the passengers survived. I came out of it with nothing more than a fractured leg." He looked over at Father Matthew and bit his lip for a moment. "I guess God still has something in store for me. It was a blessing that if the helicopter had to crash, it would happen near this village, where at least I'm being taken care of. My thanks to each and every one of you for that and for what you do for each other." He was reminded of Father Matthews appeal to give of oneself in the sermon the previous evening.

One of the younger veterans with a prosthetic leg yelled across the room, "Sir, how long did it take you to get over PTSD? I'm still having a tough time dealing with it. Does it ever go away? Seems like you've adjusted to life beyond your years in the forces." A few of the fellow veterans echoed his sentiments.

"Well, it's certainly not easy," replied Oscar. "I'll tell you what though. Just before we are about to indulge in a hearty Christmas dinner is probably not a good time to talk about it. But it looks like I am going to be here for a while." He pointed to his fractured leg in the plaster cast. "When you have time and you want to chat, just let me know."

Father Matthew smiled and said a silent prayer.

CHAPTER 15

Back at the hotel, Marilyn, Cassie, and Derek were enjoying the view of Poinsettia Plaza between fits of laughter.

"Well, I guess I should go and spruce myself up for dinner," said Marilyn, stretching to ease out of her seat. She noticed a pale blue SUV pulling up in front of the hotel. "That's the first car I've seen in the plaza today."

Derek stared out the window and saw grime and sludge all around the rims and halfway up the side panels. *The car's begging for a carwash. I wonder ... how did it get so filthy?*

Cassie leapt out of her chair. "Oh, my gosh. I can't believe it. It's my dad! How in the world did he get here?" She rushed excitedly out of the room and almost slipped on the ice-covered wooden steps. But that didn't prevent her from running to greet her father who had walked to the passenger side of the car to open both doors. Her concussion made her slightly giddy, but she didn't care. She threw her arms around him, ignoring the two female passengers getting out of the car. Instead, she basked in the hug she was receiving, even though it seemed distant. "I can't believe it, Daddy. You're here on Christmas Day! Are we going back to Cody? I thought the roads were closed. Where's Heather? Did you leave her behind?" Cassie continued to cling to him as the questions flowed effusively.

Her dad broke away, but held his hands on her shoulder. "All in good time," he said. "You're looking great, Cassie, but before we do anything, I'd like you to meet Heather."

Cassie looked at the woman who had now moved up next to her father. *Well, she's certainly very beautiful. Her eyes are the color of sapphires — and what a lovely warm, sincere smile she has.* She stretched out her arms to greet her stepmother, and whispered in her ear, "Thank you for being so instrumental in this reunion."

Heather patted Cassie gently on the back. "I just hope we'll be the best of friends," she said, her voice soft and husky. "Just give your dad some time. He's a little nervous."

Looking over Heather's shoulder, Cassie noticed another much younger lady standing alone. *That must be my stepsister.*

Cassie's father put his arm around the other passenger. "This is Rachel. I guess her father, Derek, was also on the same flight as you. He's staying at the inn too. Have you met him?"

"Met him?" Cassie was aghast. She hugged Rachel. "Your father has been a lifesaver to me these last few days. I don't know what I would have done without him. I'm just flabbergasted how all this has happened. Your dad is going to be so excited you're here. Look, he's in that glass-enclosed area." She pointed to where she, Derek, and Marilyn had spent most of their Christmas Day.

Rachel was relieved to hear her dad would be happy to see her. "Yes, I see him. He hasn't recognized me, yet. But, then, why would he? Here I am with a woolen scarf wrapped around most of my face, a knitted hoodie covering my hair, and a long winter coat. Besides, Dad wouldn't expect me to arrive in the same car as Raymond. I'm sorry, I mean your father."

"That's right," said Cassie in bewilderment. "How did you all connect? Do you know my father?" She looked at all three of the new arrivals, waving her hands in the air. "I'm so overwhelmed, I can't cope with this." Tears of joy started to stream down her face.

Raymond began to smile. He felt embarrassed by his daughter's tears. "All in good time," he repeated. "Come on, let's unpack the luggage and go inside out of this cold. Rachel, why don't you go and see your dad? I'm sure you're anxious. We'll bring in your overnight bag." He fumbled for the keys to the trunk.

As it was, Derek had been watching, but he didn't recognize his daughter, even as she climbed the stairs into the hotel.

"Let me help," said Cassie, grabbing one of the bags from the trunk. "I guess you're staying here? How long?" She looked back at Heather, who seemed relieved and pleased with the welcome she'd received from Cassie.

"There was a phone call from the hotel owner early this morning. Said her name was Gabriel. She and her husband had been monitoring the traffic conditions. The snow plows were already underway, clearing the road from Cody to Jackson Hole. They said there were rooms at the inn and that there was enough Christmas dinner for an army. If we wanted to take a chance and drive down here, they would make us welcome. They also gave us Rachel's phone number. They had called her first, and she was a little unsure of traveling by herself in her own car in case something happened, but she was happy to travel with anyone else coming down. The drive was slow. The roads are still slushy, but your dad was so anxious to spend Christmas with you. Weren't you, dear?" She turned to look at her husband.

Raymond nodded, shut the trunk, and handed Rachel's small overnight bag to his wife. "Here, honey, why don't you drop this off to Rachel while she is still in the patio with her dad? Cassie and I will check in."

Raymond and Cassie waited briefly at the registration desk. They both looked at each other absorbing the passage of time on each of their faces. The wasted years weighed heavily on the minds of both of them. Raymond still felt uneasy.

"Heather is certainly a very beautiful lady, Daddy."

"Thank you," he replied. "She takes extremely good care of me, and I try to do the same for her."

Cassie pinched herself to make sure what she was experiencing was real. Through Derek, she could now see her father in a totally different light. "I can't believe this is happening. It's turning out to be a wonderful Christmas. I have so much to tell you."

"And I have so much to share with you, Cassie." Raymond fidgeted and began scratching his head. "But first, I must apologize. I must…"

She put her finger up to his mouth to silence him as she remembered the messages of joy, peace, love, and giving from Father Matthew on Christmas Eve. "Please don't, Daddy. Please don't spoil the moment — this special moment in time."

CHAPTER 16

Rachel stood at the doorway of the covered patio, looking at the back of her father's head, wondering what was going through his mind as he stared out the window. Despite the reassurances from Cassie that her father would be thrilled to see her, Rachel was not so sure. She had felt more positive about the reunion when it was decided it would be at her home. Christmas would be on her turf — in her own festive surroundings, her husband at her side for support if needed. Now she was in neutral, unfamiliar territory. Her stomach churned as a host of memories from her childhood flooded through her mind.

After a few minutes standing at the entrance, Rachel removed her hood, ran her fingers through her hair, and headed toward her father. "Hello, Daddy," she said.

Derek immediately swung around. "Ouch," he yelled out in pain, as his fractured ribs reminded him that he still needed to move slowly. Rachel rushed to his side. "So sorry, I didn't mean to startle you. I forgot about your condition."

Derek beamed and, pushing down on the armrests of the chair, raised himself up. "Angel, what in the world are you doing here? Such a darn good surprise." He stretched out his arms to hug her.

"I guess I just wanted to wish you a Merry Christmas in person." Rachel still felt a little nervous but hugged him gently anyway.

"How did you get here?" Derek looked down at the street to see if there were any cars parked outside. "Where's Jeremy?"

Rachel pulled back and seated herself across from her dad. "He stayed home. We both thought it would be nice if you and I got to spend some time alone. The lady at the hotel arranged everything. I carpooled with a gentleman whose daughter was also in the helicopter accident. I believe her name is Cassie. I guess you've been spending a lot of time with her."

"Yes, the two of us spend most of our days together, but it's not what you're thinking." He smiled coyly.

Rachel softened and laughed a bit. "No, I'm sure it's not."

"So, do I need to go and pack?" Derek asked after a moment of awkward silence.

"Oh, no. The owners arranged for us to have dinner here, and they said I could stay overnight."

At that moment, Cassie entered the room. "Hi, there! I just came by to give you this," she said, handing a coffee flask to Rachel. "It was in the back of the car. Dad said it's yours." She turned to Derek and patted his arm on the way out. "Now, remember what we talked about. See you guys at dinner."

Rachel tilted her head. "And, just what did you guys talk about? I'm curious."

Derek reached out for his daughter's hand. "Well, you know what they say about curiosity killing the cat. Let's not talk about Cassie and me, let's talk about you and me." He lifted his hand and gently stroked her hair. Rachel put her hands in her coat pockets and allowed her father's fingers to run through her curls. "Gosh, I've missed you so much," he said.

"I missed you too," she replied softly, beginning to warm up to her father.

"And look how beautiful you are. But, then again, you always were."

"Well, I'll never be a graceful ballerina like you always hoped I would be," she said sarcastically. "Nor will I make it into the equestrian events at the Olympics — not in this lifetime, anyway. I don't like horses, and they really don't like me." She laughed with a hint of self-consciousness.

"My intent was just to expose you to the opportunities in life. All of the different things there are. It was the same with the trips overseas — I thought you would enjoy learning about different cultures."

"I know that now, Dad. But, at that time, I just wanted to be with you. I would have been happy just doing my homework and having you there to help me. I needed to be at home. It was the only security I had."

"I guess I messed up big time, didn't I? But I must have done something right. Look how you've turned out." He paused. "You and Jeremy still happy?"

"Believe it or not, it seems like we're on a permanent honeymoon, Dad. He loves me. We seldom argue. He's always there for me and supports me in everything I do."

Derek looked down. "I guess I deserved that."

Rachel took his hand and held it to her cheek. "I didn't mean it like that. It's different. When I look back, I know you did your best for me as a single dad. It was the only way you knew how. Mom sure as heck was never there for me."

"Do you ever hear from your mother?" he asked, now looking into his daughter's eyes.

Rachel shook her head. "No. I used to send her Christmas cards, but she moved and didn't give me her new address. The last two cards I've sent have both been returned. I do get Christmas cards from her. She sends the same thing every time — a card that's blank inside except for the spot where she scribbles 'Love Mom.' I can never make out the postmark, but they have Australian stamps on the envelopes. You haven't been around. Jeremy is all I have." She bit her lip as she felt the tears well up in her eyes.

Derek's eyes met his daughter's. "I don't know how I can make up lost years. I guess I can't, but I'd certainly like to try. I mean that. You're all I have. I was so excited to spend the holiday with you and Jeremy this year. And, seeing you here is better than anything I could have imagined. I love you no matter what. I always have, and I always will."

Rachel was hesitant. "Are you OK now with the fact that I married Jeremy? You always said he had no ambition."

Derek shrugged. "If he makes you happy, my precious, that's all that matters."

The tapping sound of high heels coming along the corridor made Rachel turn. Marilyn entered.

"Why, Derek, I see you have company. Will she be joining us for Christmas dinner?"

Rachel was irritated at her arrival. It annoyed her even more to think of the possible relationship between her father and the uninvited intruder. The discomfort of the situation was not lost on Derek.

"Marilyn, I'd like you to meet my daughter, Rachel. Rachel, please meet Marilyn. She was another one of the passengers in the accident the other day. She was heading to Cody to visit friends."

Marilyn stretched out her hand. "Pleased to meet you, Rachel. Do you mind if I join you for Christmas dinner?"

Rachel looked at her father. Before either of them could say anything, Gabriel entered the room. "Marilyn, there you are," she said. "Looking so festive." Meanwhile, she was sporting a bright-red, full-length skirt, a green top, and a white apron that said "Merry Christmas" in alternating red and green embroidered lettering. "My husband and I hope you will join us at our table for Christmas dinner. We'd love the pleasure of your company. Captain McFitten will also be joining us."

Gabriel's attention shifted immediately. "You must be Rachel," she said, giving a quick wink before extending her hand out. Rachel responded with a relieved smile.

Derek was baffled. "When did you two plan this? How do you know each other?"

"I just assumed she was your daughter. I know you two have some catching up to do, but don't forget the Nativity tonight at the ice rink. You're going to love it! The sleigh will be here at six o'clock to take us there." Gabriel put her arms around Marilyn, led her out of the patio area, and steered her toward the dining room.

CHAPTER 17

Cassie led her father and Heather into the dining room. She was pleased to see Captain McFitten and Marilyn sitting at a table — Marilyn with her back to the entrance. Noticing the table was set for five people, Cassie asked if she and her parents could join them.

"Bless you, Cassie. But we've been asked to have dinner with Gabriel and Mark. Their daughter Sarah will be sitting with us too."

Cassie saw Derek and Rachel and walked toward them. "I think this table's reserved for you," Derek said, pointing to the adjacent table. He stood up to shake hands with Cassie's father and his wife. "Thank you for bringing my daughter with you from Cody. It has certainly made my Christmas."

"It's the least I could do for the gentleman who saved my daughter's life," Raymond said. "I'm eternally grateful to you for that."

"Your wonderful daughter gives me too much credit." Derek chuckled and pointed to Captain

McFitten. "The real hero of the hour is the pilot. It was through his masterful handling of the helicopter that all of us survived."

Raymond turned to shake the captain's hand and thank him. "I think it was more divine intervention," the pilot said humbly. "We've all been given an extended lease on life. This Christmas has certainly been a surprise blessing for all of us."

Marilyn laughed. "You can say that again. I never expected to be having my Christmas dinner with you, Captain McFitten, that's for sure."

"Well, you don't have to. I hope you'll spend it with your family," came a recognizable voice from behind her.

Marilyn stood up and spun around. There, standing in the doorway to the dining room was her husband with his arms wrapped around their girls. He was beaming from ear to ear. *Oh, that boyish look of innocence. He's so totally naïve. He really has no clue why I was going to Cody for Christmas,* thought Marilyn.

"Richard! I can't believe you're here?"

"It took us five hours — I followed the snow plow to make sure I could get through. But we hated the idea of you being here alone. We wanted to have Christmas dinner with you."

"You drove for five hours just to be here?" Marilyn was stunned.

"It wasn't too bad, was it, girls? We sang Christmas carols and played games to pass the time."

Marilyn rose and stretched her arms out to the family. "Can we have a very gentle group hug?" The tears started to roll down her cheeks, as she felt the warmth and love of her family embrace her.

"We missed you, Mommy," the girls said in unison.

"You can't ever leave us at Christmas again," said Martha, the older daughter, looking forlornly up at her mother.

"I agree," said Richard, still smiling happily as he ran his fingers through his daughter's hair.

Gabriel entered the room from the kitchen. "Ah, it looks like your family made it in just in time, Marilyn. We set the table in the corner for the four of you."

"You knew about this all along?" asked Marilyn. "How do you and Richard know each other?"

"Oh, we don't," Gabriel replied, her face and chirpy tone very much in evidence. "Mark and I called him this morning to let him know they were clearing the roads from Jackson Hole and asked if they would make the drive to join us for dinner, which we're about to serve."

"Goody. I sure am hungry," said Julia, Marilyn's younger daughter.

Richard started toward the table. "Hush, Julia. Did you leave your manners at home?"

"I hope the accommodations are satisfactory?" Gabriel inquired.

"They're perfect, thank you. We had just enough time to freshen up."

"Can any of us help you in the kitchen?" asked Heather.

Gabriel wiped her brow. "Well, perhaps you and Rachel can help plate the food while Marilyn's two girls can be like Santa's elves and serve the plates. Would you like that?" Both girls nodded. "Sarah will show you what to do." Gabriel left and was followed into the kitchen by Rachel.

"Come on, young ladies. Let's see what we can do in the kitchen," Heather said to Julia and Martha as she led them out of the dining room.

Richard wiped the tears away from Marilyn's eyes while they sat alone at the table.

"You're probably messing up the mascara on my face," she said between sniffles, as she looked for a tissue in her purse.

"You will always look beautiful to me. I've missed you so much, my sweet. I love you."

She grabbed his hand and held it close to her cheek. "I know you do," she said gently, looking at his trusting, blue eyes. "You've always been so reliable, faithful, and dependable — a regular Rock of Gibraltar. A good husband, provider, and father."

"I'd do anything for you, Marilyn. You know that."

She smiled. "I know. Even drive five hours through slush and snow behind a plow truck just to be with me on Christmas Day."

"And to make sure you didn't spend it alone. I can't imagine anything worse than being alone at Christmas."

Marilyn suddenly thought of Eddie. *Well, I wonder what he ended up doing today. He couldn't even pick up the phone to wish me a Merry Christmas. What a jerk. What am I thinking? I'm the one who's the jerk. How could I have been such a fool? Yes, Eddie was exciting, full of surprises, and unpredictable, but he sure as heck dropped me like a used tissue. But, oh gosh ... what if he plans to surprise me too? What will I do if he shows up here out of the blue?*

She didn't have too much time to dwell on her last thought before the girls came around to deliver bread baskets to each table.

"The lady in the kitchen — you know, the one who's in charge," Julia said, setting the last bread basket down between her parents. "Well, she said that, after dinner, they're going to the ice rink to watch the Nativity. She said we're allowed to skate afterwards. Can we go? Please, can we go? The sleigh will be stopping here and will take us there. You don't even have to drive, Daddy."

Richard looked at Marilyn. "Gosh, remember when we were dating and we used to go ice skating? Now, it's our kids who do the skating."

"If you're not too tired, it would be a nice Christmas treat for the girls. Everything is so over-the-top festive in this village. You should have been with us last night."

Richard was still grinning like the Cheshire Cat. "Sure, we can go. It sounds like fun. In fact, it's a perfect family outing for Christmas night."

The girls ran back to the kitchen giggling and walked right back out with Sarah.

"Place the salads to the left of where the dinner plates will be," Sarah instructed the girls. "Watch me."

Mark entered the dining area and poured champagne for the guests.

"OK everyone," Gabriel announced in the kitchen. "If we each manage two plates, we can serve all the dinners at the same time. Take two and follow me."

"She reminds me of Mary Poppins," Martha whispered to Julia, and they both chuckled quietly.

Once they all were seated, Mark stood up. "Would anyone here like to lead us in a prayer?"

CHAPTER 18

R uth slowly placed the chocolate birthday cake, with 10 flickering flames, in front of Noel. "Time to blow out the candles and make a wish," she said. Noel inhaled as much as he could and with all the energy he could muster, extinguished them in one fell swoop. Fran, Ruth, and Solomon all applauded.

"Don't tell anyone what you wished for," admonished Solomon. "If you do, it won't come true."

Ruth started slicing the cake. "No messing around," she said, as she handed the first slice to Noel. "We don't want to be late for the Nativity."

"Do I have time to open Fran's gift?" he asked, eyeing the oblong package with curiosity.

"Why don't you do it now, while I'm cutting the cake?"

Noel jumped out of his seat. In just a matter of seconds, he had ripped the wrapping paper off and discovered there were two boxes. He removed the polystyrene protective covering from one of them and looked inside. He pulled out the base of a bedside lamp with a metal image of a smiling Jiminy Cricket with his umbrella pointing upward, holding the light bulb. Noel beamed. "Jiminy Cricket is my favorite Disney character! How did you know?" He'd forgotten his mother mentioned it the day before in the bakery.

"A little bird told me," joked Fran.

In the other box was a lampshade with bold, wavy, blue lettering. Noel mouthed the words as he read them. "If your heart is in your dream, no request is too extreme." He spun it around and continued. "When you wish upon a star, your dreams come true." They were part of the lyrics to Jiminy Cricket's signature tune. Noel put his arms around Fran, and gave her a big hug.

"Where on earth did you find such a gift?" asked Solomon.

Fran squeezed Noel's hand. "It was in a quaint little store called Noah's Novelties. It had Noel written all over it." She smiled at the youngster who was still clinging to her.

Ruth passed around the birthday cake. "Sit down and eat your cake, Noel. You've certainly been spoiled this year for Christmas and your birthday, of course. What do you say to Fran?"

The boy giggled. "Thank you, Fran."

There were bouts of laughter between each bite of cake. As soon as Noel had finished eating, his mother instructed him to run upstairs and fetch his ice-skating gear.

Solomon cleared the plates from the table. "Do you need to freshen up at all, Fran?" he asked.

"I'm fine, thanks," she replied. "Let me help clear the table."

Ruth loaded the dishwasher and heard Noel stampeding down the stairs. "Not so fast, Noel. You'll break your neck one of these days."

"Sorry", he yelled back as he picked up his new skating soakers that he left under the tree.

They all got into the car and headed off for the Nativity. As they turned onto Snowflake Way, they saw the sleigh pulling up to the ice rink a short distance down the road. Fran recognized her new friends from the Holly and Ivy Inn as she and the Hollyberrys pulled into the parking lot.

There were hugs and handshakes all around as Marilyn, Cassie, and Derek introduced their families to Fran.

"I guess a lot happened after I left today," Fran said, looking at all the new faces.

"And, these wonderful people are Mr. and Mrs. Hollyberry, who so generously sent us those beautiful baskets of goodies. And, their son, Noel, who delivered them," said Marilyn, as she ruffled the boy's head with her hand.

"It was nothing at all," said Ruth.

They all headed toward the entrance chatting effusively over the festive sleigh ride. Just outside the door was Santa ringing a bell and standing proudly in front of the Salvation Army placard. Cassie smiled. "What kind of Christmas would it be without the Salvation Army donation boxes? It's the epitome of the Christmas spirit, don't you think?"

Noel, who was holding Fran's hand, responded. "It sure is. And, did you know that every time that bell rings an angel gets its wings?"

Fran turned to the Hollyberrys who were walking arm in arm behind her. "He's so precious." They nodded and smiled.

She searched her purse for some money and stuffed it into the donation box. Solomon, Derek, and Raymond each dropped a $20 bill. "Ho-ho-ho," cheered Santa in his gruff voice to the rhythm of the bell.

"Ho-ho-ho back at ya," chuckled Noel.

"Merry Christmas, Andrew," said Ruth, as she saw the veteran stationed at his customary hot drink stand next to the Salvation Army sign. "Is it the same as before? Donate to the cause, and the drinks are free?"

"Merry Christmas, everyone," he replied, looking at the group of customers in front of him. "Same as always, Ruth — hot drinks are on the house. Help yourself. There's hot chocolate and warm apple cider. And there's cinnamon and marshmallows to top them off."

Ruth poured herself a cup of cider. "Are Mark and Gabriel here yet? We made a pact that whoever got here first would reserve a block of seats in the front for our guests."

Andrew replenished his coffee and cider from the two large urns. "Oh, sure. They arrived here about ten minutes ago — same time as Father Matthew and Oscar."

"Is that man with the bad leg here?" Noel asked. "Gee whizz, I need to go and see him. He liked my performance last night. He said I made a great Tiny Tim." As he disappeared into the arena, Solomon beckoned everyone to follow him. "Our seats are all down front. Anyone who wants to rent skates can grab them at the counter when we get inside."

"I'm impressed," said Marilyn, looking around the rink. "It has such a cozy feeling." The seats were arranged in a semi-circle and were mostly occupied, save for a few empty chairs scattered throughout. On the far side stood a small, wooden shed. It was too dark for Marilyn to see if anything was inside.

Everyone greeted Oscar with Christmas wishes, but he was preoccupied with Noel.

"How's your leg doing, Sir?" the youngster asked.

"How about you stop calling me Sir and start calling me Oscar?"

"How about I call you Uncle Oscar? I don't have any uncles."

The elderly man smiled and pinched Noel's cheek. "Sure, you can. Whatever makes you happy, young man."

"Too bad your leg is in such lousy shape. We could have skated together after the Nativity."

Oscar laughed. "No, skating's not for me. I never could do it."

"Do you like fishing?"

"Sure do."

Noel's face lit up. "Will you come fishing with me one day?"

Oscar winked. "Only on one condition. The one who catches the biggest fish doesn't have to pay for the worms."

"No deal. What about the one who catches the most fish doesn't have to pay for the bait?"

"You drive a hard bargain, son. But you got yourself a deal." Oscar pinched his cheek again.

Since no one knew of Noel's future or where he would be in February when Ruth's baby was due, Solomon was anxious about his son developing bonds and making commitments he would not be able to keep. "Stop badgering the gentleman. Come and sit down," he said, patting the seat next to him. "The show is going to start any minute now."

"Gotta run, Uncle Oscar." Oscar was taken aback as Noel gave him a firm hug, but he reciprocated. Noel climbed a couple of rows forward to where his parents and Fran were seated.

Suddenly, the lights in the stadium dimmed, and a voice boomed out of the loud speakers. "Merry Christmas, ladies and gentleman. Please give a warm welcome to the talented boys and girls of our schoolhouse who proudly present the 39th annual performance of the Nativity."

CHAPTER 19

❝**L**et's give a huge round of applause for our performers," exclaimed the deep, masculine voice of the broadcaster. The cast bowed in unison, while everyone stood to their feet, whistling and clapping loudly. "Everyone is invited to skate with the cast," he said. His voice was immediately replaced by "The Skater's Waltz" playing over the loud speaker.

Like many others, Noel hopped over the rail and took off to the rink at the speed of lightning. He peeled his shoes off, threw them in a cubby, and laced up his skates. The second his blades touched the ice, the voice returned. "I'm sure you all recognize Noel. This special young man shares the same birthday as Jesus. Let's all wish him a happy one, shall we?" He halted the music while the audience performed a heartfelt, *a cappella* rendition of "Happy Birthday."

Martha and Julia both tugged at their father's woolen scarf. "Can we go skate now? Please, Daddy," they begged.

Marilyn squeezed her husband's hands. "Go and have some fun on the ice. I'm going to sit this one out, but I'll watch."

Richard kissed his wife. "Come on, girls. Let's see what kind of skates we can get." They headed toward the rental store.

Marilyn was enthralled by the Nativity. "That was absolutely magical! I've never seen such a charming performance. The ten little boys acting as innkeepers who skated onto the ice carrying those cardboard wooden doors were so cute — especially when, one by one, they stuck their heads out and shook them to indicate there was no room in the inn."

Heather jumped in. "The real cuties in my mind were the ten little girls dressed as angels. Their adorable white outfits, wings, and halos made them look so precious. It was touching to see the five older girls holding hands with the five younger ones to help them skate. And, I couldn't help but laugh when one of them waved to someone in the audience — probably her parents."

Cassie turned to face her. "My favorite part was when the last innkeeper beckoned Joseph and Mary to the dark, dingy-looking shed, and they disappeared inside." She shook her shoulders to convey her imagined perception. "Then, when the spotlight came on, and the fresh hay was spread all over the floor … it's like you could smell it. Joseph and Mary rocked the cradle together in such a way that it looked so pure and natural. They thought of every detail — I could even see two cows laying down at the back of the shed. And, I'm not sure who that was singing 'Away in a Manger,' but she had the voice of an angel. Simply spectacular! It was such a moving experience, soaking up the atmosphere and reflecting on the true spirit of Christmas."

"Interesting," said Derek. "I thought the most moving part was immediately after the manger went dark and then the arena did too. You couldn't see the skater, but I think it was the really tall one over there." He pointed to a gentleman in black. "I guess it was a battery-operated star he was carrying on a high stick. The way he zig-zagged back and forth across the ice so slowly before hoisting the star on top of the shed." He shrugged. "I don't know. It just moved me."

Fran rubbed her shoulders to keep herself warm. "That was just before my favorite part, when the three wise men skated in from one side wearing turbans and rich, velvet-looking robes, gifts in hand. Then, from the other side, the three shepherds in their plain, gray cloaks appeared on the ice. I thought it was so clever how they alternated the verses of 'We Three Kings' and 'While Shepherds Watched Their Flocks by Night.' It can't be easy skating in those robes. What was your favorite part, Oscar?"

"I don't know about this village," Oscar said, shaking his head. "I was moved by the play and Father Matthew's service last night, not to mention the 'count our blessings' meeting earlier today. And, now, I've been moved by this too." He threw up his hands. "But the part I liked the most was at the end — when the skaters formed a circle around the edge of the rink and 'Joy to the World' started playing. All ten innkeepers skated to the middle of the ice and formed the letter 'J'." He drew the letter in the air with his finger. "And how about those angels lining up next to them, joining hands to form the letter 'O'. Then, finally, Joseph and Mary joined the three wise men and the shepherds in the shape of a 'Y', spelling JOY." He shook his head again. "I couldn't believe how quickly they rearranged their positions to spell LOVE." Everyone took note of how animated and enthusiastic Oscar was. "Oh, and the finale — when they skated their way into the word 'PEACE.' That was the ultimate. Not one of them was out of line. They're just little kids. All I can say is bravo. I haven't seen a Nativity since I was a child. This is how I always want to remember it. It was so creative and imaginative. I think I am finally discovering the Christmas spirit."

Father Matthew placed his arm on Oscar's shoulder. "I think you belong here, Oscar. I really do."

Fran was feeling pensive. *I can relate to your thought about discovering the Christmas spirit, Oscar,* she thought.

The Hollyberrys had been sitting next to Gabriel, Mark, and Sarah. "You've been doing so much cooking these last few days, which is usually your holiday week," Ruth said with a laugh. "Solomon and I would like to have everyone over for some Danish pastries, muffins, and lattes tomorrow morning — before they all head off."

Gabriel patted Ruth's hand. "That would be really nice. I'm not sure what time they plan to leave. I'm going to suggest they wait until after lunch. There's sunshine in the forecast. Hopefully, it will melt the last bit of snow and give the roads a chance to dry up, so it's not so slippery."

Solomon made the announcement about breakfast at the Hollyberrys, and everyone's face lit up.

"That will be so nice," said Fran. "We can all walk there — it's such a pretty stroll through Poinsettia Plaza. I ventured through it yesterday."

Ruth tapped the minister's shoulder. "Perhaps you can bring Oscar? And, Father Matthew, we'd love it if you could join us … if you have time."

"You're too kind," he replied.

Oscar shook his head again. "You're all too kind. I've never been anywhere like this — where everyone is so loving, so giving." Father Matthew noticed Oscar's eyes glistening, and it wasn't from the light.

Noel stopped at the railing immediately below them. "Fran, Uncle Oscar, are you watching me skate?"

Fran smiled and waved. "Yes, we're all watching you." She leaned forward to speak to Gabriel. "Is there enough room on the sleigh for me to ride back to the inn? I thought it would save Ruth and Solomon a trip."

"Sure, there's plenty. If not, you can ride back with us," replied Gabriel.

Marilyn's eyes were glued to her daughters. They were pirouetting and performing salchows with two of the innkeepers, while Richard twirled the young Mary around. *I feel like I'm in a different world, a different time zone.* She broke out of her thoughts and saw the girls tugging at Richard's sweater. She could tell they were tired from all the excitement, and smiled as she watched them return the skates to the rental booth.

A voice came over the loud speaker. "Ladies and gentlemen, boys and girls. As we bring this evening to its end, we wish you all a Merry Christmas and a safe drive home. But, before we say goodbye, you know the tradition. Everybody link arms, and sing along."

The audience became one, swaying back and forth, singing "I'm dreaming of a white Christmas." Marilyn rubbed her arms. "Oh, my goodness — I have goosebumps."

"Me too," said Cassie. "Don't know about anyone else, but, even though I don't want this to end, I'm ready to head back to the inn for some sleep. Maybe it's all this fresh air. What time does the sleigh leave?'

"Oh, the coachman stayed here. He wanted to watch the Nativity," replied Gabriel.

Julia and Martha rushed to hug their mother, and Richard followed, smiling lovingly at his wife. Noel swapped his skates out for his shoes and trudged up the steps. "Are we leaving now?" he asked.

Ruth nodded as she put her arms around him. "Come on, birthday boy." Solomon offered to assist Andrew with Oscar. Together, they lifted him out of his seat and helped him up the stairs.

Everyone said goodbye and exchanged hugs before the visitors climbed onto the sleigh.

"We'll see you at The Gingerbread House at nine tomorrow morning," Ruth yelled to everyone.

As the horses pulled away, the bells jingled. "Jingle bells, jingle bells, jingle all the way," the coachman started singing solo, but it wasn't long before the group joined in.

There were more hugs and farewells between Gabriel, Mark and the Hollyberrys as they said their goodbyes.

Fran waved at Noel from the back of the sleigh until the merry voices of the singers faded in the distance and they made their way from Snowflake Way to Candy Cane Lane. He grabbed hold of both of his parents' hands. "You know what? No one will ever replace you as parents, but, when I go to bed tonight, I'm going to follow Jiminy Cricket's advice. That lamp said 'When your heart is in your dream, no request is too extreme.' It also said 'When you wish upon a star your dreams come true.' Well I'm going to wish upon a star tonight and dream that Fran will be my new mom ... when you can't keep me any longer. I just hope and pray *my* dreams and wishes will come true."

CHAPTER 20

"Mommy, Daddy, look at that Christmas tree!" Martha and Julia raced toward the giant fir in the center of Poinsettia Plaza. "It's enormous!"

"Keep your voice down, Martha," admonished her father.

"And, walk, don't run," chastised Marilyn. "It's slippery. You don't want to fall and hurt yourself."

It was the morning after Christmas — the group chatted, laughed, and reminisced about the previous evening as they headed toward The Gingerbread House. They took their time, stopping to admire the colorful poinsettias.

"Simply beautiful," said Marilyn, as she stooped and placed her hands on a perfectly shaped poinsettia leaf. "I feel the same way as Oscar last night. I really feel as if I'm truly discovering the Christmas spirit."

"Me too," said Cassie, realizing how the helicopter accident had changed her perspective on her family and her life.

Fran tightened the scarf around her neck. "It's so nice that you can both join us," she said to Mark and Gabriel. "For once, we can chat without you having to dash back and forth into the kitchen. But it's a pity Sarah couldn't come."

"Well, someone has to keep an eye on things back at the inn. Captain McFitten is there, and he might need something," replied Gabriel, linking arms with her husband.

When they arrived at the bakery, Ruth was waiting to greet them. "Come on in, everyone. Welcome." She heard the clock tower strike nine. "You're right on time."

"Gee, Mommy, look at that awesome gingerbread house," cried Martha.

"Martha, I've already told you once to keep your voice down. Any more outbursts, and I'm taking you back to the hotel. Do you understand?" Marilyn looked fondly at Richard, appreciating his firm but gentle manner.

Oscar, Father Matthew, and Andrew were already seated at a table. Fran pulled up a chair and joined them. "Good morning. How's everybody doing today? How's your leg, Oscar?"

"Leg's getting better and less painful by the day, thank you." He patted it gently. "I guess, today, I'm just basking in the wonderful glow of Christmas."

Marilyn turned her head. "You know what, Oscar? You summed it up perfectly. If I had to describe my mood today, in light of Christmas Eve and the events of yesterday, that's exactly what I'm experiencing — the glow of Christmas."

"Me, too," said Fran. "What a beautifully apt description. Christmas has never been my favorite holiday, but, this year … this year sure is different."

Cassie laughed. "I know what you mean. Who would have thought that after surviving a helicopter crash, with all these aches and pains, that we could all have such a wonderful time?"

"Not to mention the gift of new beginnings," added Derek, wrapping his arm around Rachel's shoulder, squeezing her close to him.

Gabriel beamed. "I'm so glad you were all able to feel joy during this festive season in our little village, especially given the circumstances. After all, none of you expected to be here."

The room fell quiet while everyone became lost in their thoughts. Ruth broke the silence when she walked in holding a tray filled with assorted pastries, muffins, and donuts. She laid a platter on each of the tables. "Here you are. I hope you enjoy our freshly-baked goodies. Solomon will be out in just a second with the coffee."

"Where's Noel?" asked Fran.

"Don't worry. He'll be here shortly," replied Ruth, with a laugh in her voice. "He was watching one of the DVD's you gave him. He couldn't wait. As soon as it's finished, he's heading over."

Solomon entered the room. "Coffee anyone? I have regular here, but we have decaf too. And, if anyone wants a latte, espresso, cappuccino, or anything else, let me know — I'll be happy to make it." Ruth and Solomon sat with Gabriel and Mark. A lively conversation ensued among all in the room, as the visitors reminisced over the last few days.

When Noel finally arrived, he ran straight to Fran and wrapped his arms around her tightly. "Morning, Fran. I just finished watching one of the DVD's you bought me. I loved it!" He started to back away and remembered the crash. "Oh, Fran, I'm sorry. I shouldn't have hugged you so hard."

She smiled. "Don't worry about it, kid. I'm getting stronger every day."

"Good morning, Father Matthew," Noel said nodding toward the pastor. "And, it's good to see you,

Uncle Oscar. I can't wait until your leg's better so we can go fishing."

"It might be a while, young man. But we'll definitely make it happen, OK?" Oscar extended his hand.

"Deal," said Noel, grinning from ear to ear, and the two shook on it.

Father Matthew rose from his chair. "Well, now that your important business transaction has been settled," he said with a smile on his face, "it's time for us to head back." He and Andrew helped Oscar to his feet.

Cassie, Marilyn, and Derek also rose.

Marilyn teared up a little. Oscar didn't make a good first impression, but she had warmed up to him the last couple of days. "I guess this is goodbye," she said as she leaned over to hug him. "Do take care of yourself. When you get back to Jackson Hole, please give us a call." She reached into her purse, pulled out a business card, and handed it to him. "Perhaps you'd come over for dinner some night." Oscar was taken aback and touched by her gesture. He couldn't remember the last time he'd been invited to someone's home.

"Same goes for me," said Cassie, handing him one of her cards before giving him a hug. "And, I hope the glow of Christmas and the Christmas spirit stays with you forever."

"Rotten break, my friend," Derek said, pointing at Oscar's leg. "I don't have a card with me, but I'll send one when I get home. It would be nice if we all kept in touch. It's not every day we have life-altering experiences like this."

Andrew, Father Matthew, and Oscar said their goodbyes, thanked the Hollyberrys, and left. As the pastor closed the door, he waved and said, "I'll be over to the inn later to bid you all a fond farewell and to pray for your safe travels."

Noel ran after them. "Wait for me," he cried. "I need to tell Uncle Oscar about the different types of salmon and trout he can catch in the lake here. Boy, you should see the size of them." The group in the coffee shop all laughed as they listened to the excitement in Noel's voice.

Solomon grinned. "Unfortunately, we hear more stories from Noel about the size of the fish that got away." He put his arms around his wife. "We're sure going to miss him."

A brief silence engulfed the room.

Raymond looked at his watch. "Good heavens, that's surely not the time. It's almost noon. Come on, my sweet," he said. "We need to get back to the inn, pack our cases, and head back to Cody before it gets dark."

"My sweet? Are you referring to me or Heather?" asked Cassie, a laugh in her voice.

He pulled them in for a group hug. "Both of you, of course. And I mean it." He hugged them again. The two women looked up at him lovingly.

Heather turned to look at Derek and Rachel. "Would you like to ride back to Cody with us? There's plenty of room in the car."

"That would be mighty fine, thank you," said Derek, his diction and drawl revealing his background. "I appreciate it."

Richard patted Marilyn's hand. "I guess we should be heading back to the inn to pack too. We can head to Cody to see your sick friend. She probably needs you more than ever."

Marilyn glanced at her daughters and then at her husband. She shook her head. "No," she said. "I spoke to her yesterday," she lied. "Apparently her neighbors stopped by on Christmas Eve to see how she was doing, and, since she was alone, they invited her to spend Christmas Day with them. As long as she has someone with her, she's fine. She was just dreading being alone. Plus, I've had a crazy couple of days — I'm ready to go home." She changed the subject to avoid any further discussion on the topic. "Fran, would you like to ride back to Jackson Hole with us today? I'm sure there's room in our vehicle."

Fran's eyebrows were knitted, as if deep in thought. "You know, I think I'm going to stay a little longer. I want to chat with Ruth and Solomon about something. But I'll be back before you leave, so we'll have a chance to say goodbye."

Gabriel stood up to leave. "Captain McFitten told me his company was arranging transportation for him to leave here tomorrow. He's going back to Jackson Hole, so I'm sure you could ride back with him, Fran, if you'd like to stay an extra night with us."

Fran nodded and smiled. *She always seems to have all the answers. So warm and reassuring. What a loving person.* Gabriel walked out, leaving Solomon, Ruth, and Fran alone in the coffee shop.

CHAPTER 21

"Let me help you clean up," said Fran, as she started to stack the empty plates on her table.

Ruth laughed. "Thank you. Normally, we wouldn't let guests help us, but I feel like you're almost family." She loaded as many dishes as her tray would hold and left for the kitchen. Solomon wiped off all the tables she had cleared.

Fran was just biding her time until everything was back to its pristine condition. She seated herself at a table near the window, so she would be able to see when Noel was on his way back from the Heavenly Home for Disabled Veterans.

"Is there something you wanted to discuss with us?" asked Ruth, as she and her husband joined their guest at the table.

Fran looked back and forth at the two of them and took a deep breath. "I don't know how you're going to take this news, but ... I'd like to adopt Noel." She held her hands up to stop them from saying anything before she finished. "I've had a lot of time to think since I've been in this village. I gave the matter a lot of thought on Christmas morning, and I was awake most of last night thinking about it. In fact, 'twas the night before Christmas that I actually started thinking about it. I had my own visit from Saint Nicholas." She laughed nervously at her own joke. "Of course, I know that with any adoption, the child has to give their approval. I just hope that Noel will want to come and live with me."

Ruth reached across the table to squeeze Fran's hand. "Why, that's absolutely wonderful news! The best Christmas gift any of us could ask for!" She looked at her husband. "Don't you agree, Solomon?"

He rose and moved around the table to give Fran a hug. "It is. It's spectacular news. And, you don't have to worry about Noel. He'll be elated. There are no plans for Noel at this point. Ruth and I knew the right person would appear at the right time. We'll help you as much as we can, especially with Child Support Services of Wyoming. The paperwork is a minefield."

"Yes, dear," replied Ruth. "But our case worker can help. We can help get the process expedited. Maybe she knows someone at the agency in Jackson Hole." She turned back to Fran. "I'm so excited. Since you live so close, maybe you can still bring Noel to visit us from time to time? Neither of us can bear the thought of not seeing him again."

"Well, actually, I was thinking of moving here. But I wasn't sure how difficult it would be to find a place to rent or buy in this small village, or how I'd even go about it."

Ruth couldn't contain her excitement. "Oh, there's only one place that handles properties here. It's Rudolph's Real Estate. We can certainly arrange for you to meet the owner, Rudy. He's such a nice gentleman. But what about your job? Your career?"

"No need to worry about that. I'm a financial advisor, so I'm either on the phone or my computer — I work from home. Since I can bring my job here with me, there shouldn't be any issues getting approved for a loan."

Ruth clasped her hands. "Fran, you're a saint. The answers to my prayers."

Solomon grinned. "Well, I don't know about a saint, but you certainly are an angel. Moving here will definitely make it easier. You'll probably have the same case worker as we do. She adores Noel. We see her every month, and I'm sure she'll do everything she can to make things happen as quickly as possible. You'll have to be his foster parent first. It'll take a little longer for him to be adopted. His parents passed, so he's essentially a ward of the state. But it's all doable."

Fran was relieved at the support she was receiving. "I did think long and hard," she reiterated. "I thought it would be too disruptive to move him away from his school and everyone he knows. Besides, it will be nice for him to be near you guys — you've been his family for so long. It made sense for me to uproot my life instead of making Noel do it. When I first met him, he told me he'd been in and out of foster homes. Hopefully, by filing adoption papers, he'll have security. I'm so happy you'll both be here to help me."

The tears started to roll down Ruth's face. "You're so thoughtful. You're already putting Noel first. What about your friends? Won't you miss them?"

Fran shrugged. "People make friends wherever they are in the world. And, everyone in this town is so welcoming. Just look at the memories we've made in a few short days. But, before we get ahead of ourselves, when is the next visit from your case worker? I'd like to be here for it."

"The first week in January. I have to check my calendar for the exact date," said Ruth, wiping away her tears with her apron.

"Well, then — tomorrow I'll take that ride back to Jackson Hole with Captain McFitten. When I come back in January, I'll meet with the case worker and get the ball rolling with the paperwork. Meanwhile, if you give me Rudy's number, I'll contact him. Hopefully, he can show me some homes while I'm here." Fran looked at her watch. "Oh, dear! I should be getting back to the inn to say goodbye to everyone. They must be getting ready to leave now, and I'd hate to miss them. Besides, I've already taken up so much of your time." She rose to leave.

"I'm looking forward to celebrating more birthdays, Christmases, and holidays with you and Noel," said Ruth, giving Fran a big hug.

"That goes for me, too," said Solomon. "We can't wait to tell Noel the news."

"For all of us to tell him the news," said Ruth.

Fran looked at her watch. "Well, it might be better if the news came from the two of you. I think that would be nice for him. He may have reservations that he feels more comfortable discussing with you. He and I will have plenty of time to get to know each other. Besides, I need to get back to the inn, make some important phone calls, and say goodbye to my new friends — who knows when Noel will be back."

"That's not a problem. We can call Father Matthew and have him send Noel back here immediately," said Solomon.

Fran shook her head. "No, please don't do that. He's probably bonding with Oscar, which is good for both of them. If you tell Noel, I think he'll be more comfortable. I'll call him when I get back to Jackson Hole. We can have a long chat. By then, I'm sure he'll have tons of questions." She picked up one of their business cards from the counter and handed hers to Solomon. "I'll be calling you with questions, I'm sure. And you call if you have any for me, OK? I know there's much more we need to discuss." She tightened the scarf around her neck. "I can't thank you enough for your kindness. I'm not sure what time Captain McFitten is leaving tomorrow morning. I might not see you again."

They hugged each other again, and Fran left. As soon as the door to the coffee shop closed, Ruth reached into her apron pocket and fumbled around for her cellphone.

"Heavenly Home for Disabled Veterans."

"Thank goodness you answered the phone, Father. It's Ruth. You know Fran, the lady that sat with you this morning? She wants to adopt Noel. Oh, Father, Solomon and I are so excited! Noel really loves her."

"Yes, I can see that. I noticed it last night at the ice rink."

"He told us when we got home that he wanted her to be his new mom. Please, Father, I just called to ask you to pray that this transpires."

"Say no more," replied the minister. *An unexpected turn of events,* he thought. *But a most welcome one.* "Noel and Oscar were out on the patio talking nonstop about fishing. I just sent him home a few minutes ago, so you can expect him any second."

"Yes, he's coming. I can see him dragging his feet down the street with hands in his pockets as usual. Thank you, Father."

As soon as Noel entered the shop, they broke the news.

"Wow," he hollered. "Jiminy Cricket was right. When you wish upon a star, your dreams do come true. I prayed and dreamed and wished for this." He hugged his parents, looked around and noticed Fran was not there. "Where's Fran? Where is she?"

"She had to go back to the inn to say goodbye to everyone. She's leaving tomorrow to go back to Jackson Hole. She'll be coming back next month to meet the case worker," said Ruth, stroking his hair.

Noel wrested himself from his folks. "I must go and thank her." He ran out the door, letting it slam behind him.

"Noel, you'll trip and hurt yourself," yelled Solomon following him out the door. "Noel, come back at once!" As loud as it was, his voice fell on deaf ears. Noel was on a mission, and he was already out of sight.

CHAPTER 22

Father Matthew hung up the phone. *This is all coming together beautifully.* He headed for the back porch, hoping to find Oscar. Sure enough, there was his newest resident wrapped up, keeping warm, his injured leg stretched out on the chaise lounge.

The minister pulled up a chair and sat down. "Have you given any more thought to staying here even after your leg has healed, like we discussed?"

"Yes, Father. Believe it or not, I have. But I don't really think I could be of much use here. I mean, not when it comes to helping people with PTSD, anyway."

"Well, that's not the only reason to stay. I've noticed how attached Noel has become to you, and I might suggest, as you have to him."

Oscar chuckled. "Can you believe he calls me uncle? I don't have any nephews or nieces. I was an only child. Geez, I don't even have any kids of my own. I've never been married."

"The two of you get along quite well. You probably don't know this, but the Hollyberrys are Noel's foster parents. His real parents died in a car accident. At the end of February, when Ruth gives birth to her fourth child, Noel is supposed to move in with a new set of foster parents. They could ship him off anywhere."

For a moment, Oscar was speechless. "I had no idea. That poor little kid. He's always so chirpy, and he doesn't know what's going to happen to him in two months? He must be terrified inside."

"Another reason to count our blessings, right?"

Oscar nodded. "Sure is. But why are you telling me all this, Father?"

"As it happens, Fran has stepped up to the plate and offered to adopt Noel. Not only that, she's moving here to make the transition easier on him."

"What? That's impossible. Surely she would have said something this morning while we were all having coffee."

"She wanted to talk to Ruth and Solomon first. She discussed it with them after we all left. Ruth called me after to tell me the news and ask me to pray for everything to go smoothly."

Oscar shrugged. "There's no reason to think it will."

"Oh, it will. It will. I believe it is God's will."

Oscar looked at the minister with skepticism.

"I know what you're thinking, Oscar, but as the hymn says, 'God Moves in a Mysterious Way.' And, that's exactly what's happening here."

"Oh, don't start up with all that nonsense, Father. It's pure happenstance. Nothing else. I hope it materializes for Noel, and for Fran. She's a good woman."

"Fran's going to be a single mom. And Solomon is going to have to spend more time at the shop while Ruth stays home with the baby. You could certainly be a steady hand for the boy, and be a good father figure."

"You're not trying to be a matchmaker and pair me up with Fran, are you?"

Father Matthew laughed. "Of course not."

"Good. Because I'm old enough to be her father too."

"You have to admit, Oscar, you've changed since you arrived here."

Oscar lit a cigarette. "I'll give you that, Father. And I have you to thank for it. You allowed me to unload my burden, and see things through a different prism." He became somber.

"You're a good man, Oscar. You're honest, decent, and you have good values. You've definitely got a conscience — otherwise, you wouldn't have carried your guilt around for all these years. These are sound qualities that would help Noel, and I'm sure Fran would be grateful."

"That's all well and good. But what will I do when Noel's at school?"

"How do you normally pass the time when you're in Jackson Hole?"

"I read a lot, play solitaire, watch TV. I don't know. The time just goes. I'm retired."

"I think you could put your time to a lot better use. I help with the spiritual needs of the veterans here, but not all of them are comfortable talking to a minister. They'll respect you. They'll look up to you. You can talk to them. Maybe you could help me out with some of the activities. Perhaps start a book club, host a card tournament, show your favorite movies. You could even audition to play Scrooge in next year's play."

"Now you're just laughing at me."

"No, I'm laughing with you. There's a difference. We can't pay you, but we can offer you free meals while you're here. When you're fully recovered, we'll help you find an apartment. I'll even let Andrew use the truck to collect your belongings from Jackson Hole."

Oscar suddenly realized the possibilities. This was a chance for a new life. He winked at the minister. "Do you think Fran would cook me a homemade dinner occasionally — when Noel and I come back with some fresh fish?"

Father Matthew laughed as he rose from his seat. "I'm heading over to the inn now to say goodbye to the rest of the passengers and wish them safe travels. I'll ask Fran about that dinner. There's no doubt in my mind, she'll agree. She's just a good soul." He stretched out his hand. "Do we have a deal?"

Oscar thought for a moment. "As long you don't try and make a religious soldier out of me, Father." He winked again, and they shook hands. "You've got yourself a deal."

*****

Everyone turned when they heard Noel approaching the inn. "Fran, wait!" he yelled between labored breaths. "Fran!" He was running across the plaza, his arms flailing wildly in the air. Fran hadn't mentioned her new plans to anyone. With so much confusion about who was sitting where and the endless juggling to fit all the luggage in the trunks, she hadn't had the chance. *Well, I guess the secret will be out now — the look on his face tells me he knows and he can't wait to blurt it out.*

Sure enough, Noel ran up to the steps and threw his arms around Fran. "Thank you, Fran. Thank you for wanting to be my new mom," he gushed breathlessly. "Are you really going to adopt me?"

Fran hugged him back. "That's what we're hoping for, if you approve."

"Approve?" Noel asked. "Oh, Fran, this is all I ever wished for."

Everyone cheered with excitement.

Noel looked up. "Will I come to live with you in Jackson Hole?"

"Didn't they tell you? I'm moving here. That way, you can still see your friends at school and visit with the Hollyberrys. And, if your Uncle Oscar sticks around, you can go fishing all summer long."

Gabriel stepped forward. "My dear, I think that's absolutely wonderful. Mark and I will help you in any way we can. You'll soon feel at home in our village."

Fran smiled. "I already do."

Marilyn walked over to Fran and embraced her. "Congratulations. How our lives have changed since we met at the airport a few days ago."

"Your life too?" Fran hugged her new friend.

"Yes, it really was the best Christmas ever. I realized that I have all the gifts I need — my precious little girls and my sweet husband. I missed them so much when they weren't here." She pointed to Richard, who was wiping his windshield while Martha and Julia played in the snow.

As everyone gathered around Fran to wish her well, Derek pulled Cassie aside and held her hand. "I hope your reunion with your dad and Heather was as magical as mine was with Rachel. I owe it all to you. You made me see her for the beautiful human she is rather than the daughter I wanted her to be. We talked for ages after we got back last night. I'm so proud of who she's become. I just regret the wasted years."

Cassie squeezed his hands. "You don't owe me anything. You're the one who saved my life, allowing me to reconnect with my father before I pass into the next one." She grinned. "It was through your wisdom that I was able to reevaluate my opinion of my dad. I can never, ever repay that debt of gratitude."

"Consider us square, my friend." They hugged.

Marilyn, Richard, and the girls walked over to Gabriel and Mark to express their appreciation.

"We've thoroughly enjoyed having you stay with us," said Gabriel. "I hope you'll come back and visit us in the summer months."

"Well, we certainly have good reason to with Fran staying here. Not to mention, we'd love to see the Hollyberrys and Father Matthew again."

Father Matthew parked his car behind Richard's.

"Getting lazy are we, Father Matthew?" asked Mark, with a laugh. "You're only a couple of blocks away."

"I got waylaid by Oscar, and I wanted to make sure I was here to say goodbye and wish you all a safe journey home. I thought if I walked, I might miss you." He turned to Fran and clasped her hands in both of his. "Congratulations. I heard the news about you adopting Noel."

"Wow, news does travel fast, doesn't it?" asked Fran.

The minister laughed. "Well, you're moving to a small town, so you might as well get used to it. Oscar's decided to stay in the village, too, so he can be a sort of father figure to Noel — if you feel comfortable with that, of course."

Fran was startled. "You're not trying to play matchmaker, are you?"

"Not at all. Oscar asked the same thing. But he did say he'll take an occasional dinner invite if Noel comes home with fresh-caught fish."

"I'll gladly do that," Fran replied. "Actually, I'm quite fond of the old guy. But I certainly don't have any romantic inclinations toward him."

Marilyn turned to Gabriel and Mark. "I guess we'll need to add Oscar to the list of reasons to return in the summer." She extended her hand to the pastor. "I'll never forget your message to us on Christmas Eve, Father Matthew. I thank you for that. It was a life-altering experience for me. A real moment of truth."

Cassie suggested they have a summertime reunion in Christmas Carol Village and everyone agreed.

Father Matthew climbed into his car. "Come on, Noel," he said. "Get in. I'll drop you off at the coffee shop."

Noel gave Fran another huge hug. "Can't wait to see you again," he said, and jumped into the passenger seat.

Fran waved goodbye and went inside.

Mark and Gabriel stood on the sidewalk, looking out over Poinsettia Plaza. It was all so quiet and serene.

"This has been quite a Christmas. I wonder what next year will bring," Gabriel said softly to her husband.

"I suppose it will be whatever our creator has planned for the universe," Mark replied.

They turned around, and with their arms around each other, they walked slowly up the steps to the inn.

TO MY READERS

Thank you so much for taking the time to read this novel, which I hope gave you much reading pleasure.

If you enjoyed my book, I would be most grateful if you would consider submitting a review to any or all of the following:–

- My website at
  www.discoveringthechristmasspirit.com
- Amazon at www.amazon.com
- Goodreads at www.goodreads.com
- For a complete list of other novels I have written, please visit my author website at
  www.authorstephenmurray.com
- Happy reading!

Stephen Murray

stephen@casandras.net

Made in the USA
Middletown, DE
23 August 2022

71298950R00106